meow
or
never

meow
or
never

Jazz Taylor

Scholastic Inc.

All rights reserved. Published by Scholastic Inc., *Publishers since 1920.* SCHOLASTIC and associated logos are trademarks and/or registered trademarks of Scholastic Inc.

The publisher does not have any control over and does not assume any responsibility for author or third-party websites or their content.

This book is a work of fiction. Names, characters, places, and incidents are either the product of the author's imagination or are used fictitiously, and any resemblance to actual persons, living or dead, business establishments, events, or locales is entirely coincidental.

ISBN 978-1-338-68468-1

10 9 8 7 6 5 4 3 2 1   21 22 23 24 25

Printed in the U.S.A.   40

First printing 2021

Book design by Yaffa Jaskoll

To **Grandma**, with love,
and to all the girls who are afraid
but conquer the world
anyway

Chapter 1

Today is an important day. Two reasons: One, it's the first day back to school after winter break.

And two, I'm about to make my first friend.

Well, it won't technically be my *first* friend. It's just my first one since we moved here. Even though that was six months ago. The beginning of seventh grade was pretty rough.

I've been planning all week. I'm wearing the new red sweater Dad got me for Christmas, and I scrubbed my tennis shoes so they *look* new, even though they aren't. I pulled my curly black hair into a high bun (so I won't tug on it while we talk). I murmur my practiced lines: "How was your break?" "What'd you get for Christmas?"

I breathe in the cold air at the bus stop. I can't believe it's so cold in northern Alabama! I moved from southern Alabama, so I'm not used to this. I shift from foot to foot and adjust my sweater nervously. I can say something that simple, surely. My palms sweat inside my old gloves, so I take them off and stuff them into my pocket. I'm all set. I'm going to do it. The next person who walks up to me, I'll talk to. And we'll be friends, and I won't have to sit in the back of the theater at lunch, and maybe we can even hang out after school sometimes when Dad has to work late—

My excitement dries up in an instant. Because the next person who walks up to the bus stop is Nic Pearson. Nic, the girl who makes everyone laugh, who is pretty and kind, who makes my chest get this funny feeling when she meets my eyes.

Nic, the girl I made a complete and utter fool of myself in front of last semester.

I give up. No friends this year.

"Avery, hey!" Nic runs the last few feet to meet me, smiling with her perfect teeth and cute light brown freckles under her eyes. She's taller than me by a few inches, and her skin is a lighter shade of brown than mine. She stands next to me, uncomfortably close. "How was your break? What'd you get for Christmas?"

No, these are my lines! My mouth is dry, but my hands, my back, under my arms are so sweaty. What do I do?

Nic is waiting for me, still smiling. Okay, I can do this. I know what I got for Christmas. A new sweater. A case for my phone. A stuffed cat Dad thought was cute.

Come on, I will myself. *Say you got a new sweater. You can do this.*

But I can't do this. All I can think about is our last conversation, and about how she hangs out with all the other drama kids, so she doesn't need a weirdo like me, and I don't say anything. I don't say a word as Nic's smile fades and she looks away and the bus arrives and I sit in the back and wish the world would swallow me whole.

"Class, come here," Mrs. Thompson calls us from the stage. I look up from my doodling. It's seventh period, the last one of the day, and I somehow survived.

Nic is in *three* of my classes, so I've been avoiding her. After my embarrassing display this morning, I would rather die than have her look at me like I'm a weirdo who can't talk. She's in this class too, so I wait for her to go to the stage before joining everyone at the back.

Mrs. Thompson beams at us. She's tall and thin, and her bright green dress clashes with her pale skin. Like a festive vampire. Except that she's a nice teacher, always smiling, always wearing a new streak of color in her hair. Today the strip is bright pink.

"I hope we all had a good break, but now we need to talk about this semester's play."

"We just did one," Thomas complains. He's usually in the cast, based on the play we did last semester, but he acts like he doesn't even *like* theater.

"And we'll do another!" Mrs. Thompson says, laughing. "This time will be a little different. Come up here, Harper."

A girl with blonde hair, light skin, and brown eyes climbs the steps to the stage and stands beside Mrs. Thompson.

She's tiny! And nervous. She's picking at the hem of her shirt, something I do too.

"I'm sure y'all know Harper. But in case you don't, here she is!"

Poor Harper looks like she's going to die of embarrassment. Her neck and ears are bright red. Adults really need to learn to leave kids alone.

"Harper has won an award for her script, and I think it would be nice to perform it, don't you?"

Mrs. Thompson phrases it as a question, but she's looking at us like she dares us to disagree. But I think it'll be cool. At my old school, we did classic plays like *Alice's Adventures in Wonderland* and *The Wizard of Oz*. And even here, last year we did *A Christmas Carol* (which I'd already done before). I like those plays okay, but everyone knows those stories. It'll be nice to do something new. I wonder what she wrote.

"What's the play?" Nic asks, her hand raised high.

Mrs. Thompson glances at Harper, but Harper looks

close to fainting. My stomach twists in solidarity. Someone save her, please.

"It's a modern version of *Romeo and Juliet*," Mrs. Thompson finally says. "It's about two rival donut shop owners and their kids, who fall in love."

Thomas rolls his eyes, but I like it. Maybe they'll bring us donuts to get in character.

"We'll start right away! It'll involve quite a bit of singing, so we'll hold auditions over the next few days. Come to my office if you'd like to try out for the cast. Anyone who doesn't want to be in the cast can start brainstorming about sets. Any questions?"

Several hands go up, but I don't bother. I like singing (well, I really love singing), but I don't like acting. That was fine at my old school because we could pick two electives. I could sing in choir and do the crew for plays. But here you can only pick one, and I chose theater. And I don't mind! I like being behind the scenes, setting up lights and painting sets and making sure the actors are in the right place.

But still, I get a tiny prick of longing as Mrs. Thompson answers questions. I wish I could sing without having to act.

Mrs. Thompson passes out scripts and finally releases poor Harper from her torture. I watch as she hurries out of the auditorium. I know that was terrible, standing up there in front of everyone. I think about talking to her, because I get nervous too, but I don't know what I'd say.

"Okay, everyone!" Mrs. Thompson is beaming again. "We have six weeks. Let's make this *shine*."

They'll make it shine. I'll be in the back, staying out of everyone's way.

I'm not at home yet, but soon! Sorry, angel! But when I get there, I promise we'll do pizza.

I stare at Dad's text, then pull out the script from my backpack. I'm still in the auditorium, but everyone's gone home already. I don't feel like going home. No one's there anyway.

This happens a lot. Since we moved here last summer,

Dad's been really busy. He says it's good, because he makes more money now, and he wears suits instead of jeans, and we live in a house instead of an apartment. But I liked the apartment. I liked the jeans. I liked coming home knowing he was waiting for me.

I put my earbuds in to drown everything out and pick a Beyoncé song. She's my favorite artist, especially her new album, but I love almost all music. I love hearing each note, picking out harmonies and singing each part of a song until I've memorized every note, every gasp, every tick of a metronome. Even the super-low notes I can't sing so well. Dad says I should have picked choir instead of theater, but he doesn't get it. Being in the crew means I don't have to be sweaty and nervous before a concert. I can sing by myself.

I bob my head to the heavy beat as I read Harper's script. It's short, only three acts. Not bad. I pencil in what sets we'll need for each scene, and sometimes I even laugh. Romeo is a goofball who likes to play guitar, and Juliet rides a skateboard and likes anime. I can't believe someone my age wrote this. Harper's a genius!

One scene is in an alleyway behind Juliet's donut shop—I think we have an alley set already from a previous production. I definitely don't want to make another one if I don't have to. I climb to my feet, pocketing my phone, and go to the back of the stage, where all the old sets are kept. I poke around for a while but don't find it. Maybe in the closet? I open the door and stare down at my feet.

There's a cat in here.

It's a gray cat with big, round amber eyes. Its fur is short and a little dirty. The cat blinks up at me, then purrs and circles my legs. I'm too shocked to move. What's a cat doing in a closet?

I shine my phone flashlight at the back of the closet, and there's a cat-sized hole at the back, a small tunnel, and the faint glow of the afternoon sunlight.

"You came in from outside?" I ask the cat. It just purrs. I reach down to pet it, but hesitate. I've never had a cat before. Dad is afraid of them and my brother, Andrew, is allergic to cats *and* dogs. It bumps my hand with its head. Its fur is soft. And cold.

"Are you all by yourself?" I crouch and pet the cat under its chin. It purrs louder and louder. All alone.

Just like me.

The cat flops onto its side, its paws batting at my knee, and I can't help smiling at it. It's so cute. And if it's coming in here out of the cold, maybe it doesn't belong to anyone?

Maybe I can keep it?

My phone buzzes, and I look down.

Coming home early! Thin crust or pan?

"Uh oh, gotta go." I pack my script and pet the cat one more time. "I'll be back tomorrow, okay? Promise. Will you still be here?" It blinks sleepily at me, then returns to the closet. It curls up on top of a cardboard tree. I'll take that as a yes. I hop off the stage and head home, but all I can think about is that maybe I can make a friend after all.

Chapter 2

Dad pushes the Pizza Hut box across the dining room table. "I got you pepperoni, thin crust," he says, grinning. I smile back. This is the only way to eat pizza.

"What'd you get me?" Andrew asks, not looking up from his phone. Andrew is super tall, like Dad, but he's slouched in his chair so much he's almost my height. He looks a lot like Dad, except he's really thin instead of muscular, and he has a bunch of pimples on his chin. Still, everyone can tell he's Dad's son. I apparently look like a mom I've never met, so a lot of my classmates are shocked when they see Dad come to school events.

"You didn't answer my text, so nothing!" Still, Dad opens a second pizza box and reveals supreme. Gross.

"How was school?" Dad asks, glancing at both me and Andrew. Andrew eats a slice of pizza, still looking at his phone, so I answer Dad first.

"Good." I think of what happened after school and put down my pizza. "Dad, do you think we could get a cat?"

Dad almost chokes on his food. "What? You know good and well I'm not letting no cat in my house."

Well, that's out. I sigh and pick a pepperoni off my slice. I feel bad for the theater cat. It's all alone, night and day. And it was cold.

Dad frowns at me. "Why the sudden interest in cats?"

"It's 'cause she still has no friends," Andrew grunts. I throw the pepperoni at him, and he finally looks up to glare at me.

"Drew." Dad's voice is sharp. He looks back at me, his eyes soft and kind. "Avery, don't mind him. It's okay if you haven't found the right friend group yet. Don't worry."

"I'm not worried," I say, but I can't look at Dad. I wish I knew what to do to make myself talk. I just can't do it. I get nervous and sweaty and I feel like my heart will explode. Dad says it's normal to be nervous. Andrew says I'm pathetic. I don't like Andrew very much, but I'm starting to think he's right.

Dad has that look on his face, the one parents get. Like he knows more than I do. "Have you talked to anyone in your drama group? I bet they'd love to be your friend, if you asked."

Talking is the problem. "You can't just ask people to be your friend, Dad. Plus, everyone has their own group already. It's okay."

"You've gotta make opportunities for yourself. Oh, what about singing? Maybe you could try out for the play, like an acting part, not just the crew. You're bound to meet new friends that way."

As if I hadn't thought about that already. I wish he wouldn't talk about this. I don't even want my pizza anymore.

After a long silence, Dad says, "Maybe you're right. We need a pet. Something hypoallergenic so Andrew won't be sneezing."

"She can get whatever she wants next year," Andrew says. "I'll be outta here soon."

"Oh, really?" Dad's gone all big and puffy, and I know it'll be a fight. "Have you applied for any scholarships? Looked into the grants like I told you? I know you think you got it made, getting into UAB, but a full ride still ain't free."

Andrew is the opposite of Dad, all limp and surly in his chair. He doesn't look up from his phone. "You got money now, right? Since you moved us all the way out here to the sticks and bought this house."

I push away from the table before the fighting starts. "I'm going to my room," I announce, but Dad is already yelling at Andrew about disrespect and his bad attitude, so I just go upstairs.

I get ready for bed, singing in the shower loud to drown out their fighting. We never used to fight when we lived in the apartment. Dad and Andrew got along, and I had friends (well, one friend who doesn't talk to me anymore), and everything was just better. I wish Dad had never taken this dumb suit job. I wish we'd never moved.

When I'm in my pajamas, my hair wrapped carefully in a silk hat, there's a knock on my door. "Avery? Can I come in?"

Dad. I bury my face in my pillow. "Okay, I guess."

I hear the door open and feel Dad's weight on my bed. He pats my back, his hand warm and heavy.

"I'm sorry for arguing at the table, Avery. Definitely not cool."

"It's okay. Andrew's a jerk."

"Don't say that about your brother." Dad hesitates, just for a second. "Andrew is just going through a hard time. We all are. And me losing my temper isn't making it any easier."

I peek at him with one eye. He's looking down at his feet. His face is so sad.

"Do you really want me to try out for the play?"

"I think it would help you make friends! You have a lovely voice, and you should share it with everyone. You've just gotta get out of this shy spell."

A spell that's lasted my whole life. I can't look Dad in

the eye, but say, "Well, I don't need to try out, and I don't need friends. You don't have to worry about me. I'm okay. Promise."

Dad looks at me and he's still sad, but it's a different kind of sad that makes his brown eyes soft like he's going to cry. "We can get a pet if you want, Avery. How about a turtle?"

I don't want a turtle. I want a friend. But . . . the theater cat might be there tomorrow. Maybe I don't need a pet at home.

"I'm okay, Dad," I say, covering myself with my comforter, my heart fluttering with excitement. "I think I've figured something out."

The next day, I think about the gray cat all through my classes. During theater, I watch the closet door, but no one even comes close to it. As soon as the bell rings and the theater's empty, I go straight to the closet.

The cat is still there, blinking against the sudden light. It purrs and rubs its body against my hands. I breathe a sigh of relief.

"Okay, cat," I say, petting its back. "I've decided. I'm gonna take care of you, and then Dad won't worry and I won't need a friend. Deal?"

The cat flops onto its back, still purring. Sounds like a deal to me.

I sit down and pull out the things I bought at the pet store on the way to school. A pink cat bed and two shiny bowls with little paw prints at the bottom. It cost me a whole year's allowance, and I didn't even get food this time! Cats are expensive. More expensive than turtles, that's for sure.

I put the bed on top of the cardboard where the cat sleeps, and the food bowls a little closer to the hole to the outside. I read online that you're supposed to keep everything separate. I pour water from my water bottle into one of the bowls while the cat sniffs the edge of the bed, its ears pricked.

"It's okay! It's for you." Carefully, I pick up the cat and put it in the bed. The cat is heavier than it looks.

The cat sniffs the bed a few more times, then flops onto its side, purring. I guess that's a yes to the bed.

"You're pretty fat for a stray," I tell the cat, sitting beside it. The cat climbs out of the bed and into my lap, its warm weight calming me. "If we're gonna be friends, I should probably give you a name. Are you a boy or a girl?"

I pick up the cat to look at its belly, but all I can see is a lot of dirty gray fur. "I guess you can be a girl, I don't know. What do you think about Phantom? Because you live in the back of the theater and no one knows. Boys and girls can be Phantoms."

The cat blinks at me, and I put her down in my lap. She yawns and closes her eyes. Phantom it is.

Phantom and I sit together for a long time, and she seems happy napping while I do my homework. Eventually, it starts to get dark outside and all my homework is done. I close my math book and put her back into her bed. Phantom meows loudly when I stand up.

"Sorry, gotta go. But I'll be back tomorrow. And I'll bring food this time, promise."

She meows in response and I smile. I give a wave to Phantom and close the closet door.

I put my earbuds in and shoulder my backpack, swaying with the music. I walk in time with the beat, humming. For the first time since moving, I can't wait to come back to school.

Chapter 3

Lunch is the hardest part of the day.

It used to be math, because honestly math makes no sense at all and it's cruel that we have to learn it (everyone has calculators on their phones anyway!). But since I moved, lunch is the worst.

The big cafeteria is crowded already, so crowded I want to choke. Kids stream in from the hallway beneath the colorful banners announcing school events and fundraisers. Sometimes I chicken out and just drink a lot of water for lunch, but not today. Today I have to get a turkey sandwich so I can give half of it to Phantom.

I stand far behind the last kids in line, which is fine because everyone is talking to someone else anyway. I grab a turkey sandwich from the bar, along with a fruit cup, and carry it to the lunch lady. She punches in my lunch number, and I can breathe again. I did it. Now, to the theater.

I'm almost out of the cafeteria when I stop. There's Harper, the girl who wrote the play. She's sitting at a lunch table at the very back of the cafeteria.

She's sitting all by herself.

I look at the door and then back to Harper. She's writing something in a notebook, not eating anything, her blonde hair covering her face. I look at my sandwich. My hands are sweaty again.

Okay. I have two options. I can go and hang out with Phantom. Or I can sit with Harper. I can tell her I get nervous too, and the best way to stand in front of a crowd is to recite the lyrics to your favorite song or think about what you'll have for dinner. I can tell her I like her play.

I can attempt to make a *human* friend.

I take a step toward her, but suddenly I'm frozen. The disastrous conversation with Nic from the start of the year plays in my mind, and the one at the bus stop. And then I'm turning around and running out of the cafeteria, sweating like mad, gasping for air.

At least cats can't tell if you're a weirdo.

"I ruined it," I groan to Phantom. She's not listening—she's tearing into my turkey sandwich like she's never had anything to eat in her entire life. I let her have as much as she wants. I'm not hungry anymore.

"She was right there. All I had to say was 'I like your play.' And I do! It's funny!"

I roll over and scream into my backpack. It's a little louder than I intended. My pillow at home is better at hiding the sound.

I roll to my back again. We're sitting together, beside Phantom's closet. Dusty ceiling and dark stage lights are all I can see. "Why can't I just talk, Phantom? They're always right there. Right in front of me. But I can't do it."

After Phantom is done eating my sandwich, she climbs onto my stomach and tucks her paws beneath her, purring. I scratch behind her ears, a little less miserable.

"At least I have you."

I check my phone. Still ten minutes until lunch is over. I put one earbud in my ear and touch the YouTube app. I pick a soft song, humming at first, then full-blown singing as the beat picks up. Phantom listens, her ears pricked, purring. I can feel her rumbling on top of my stomach.

Suddenly, in the middle of my third song, Phantom stiffens and charges off me, running into the closet and disappearing into the tunnel. I sit up, frowning. "Where are you going? Was my singing that bad?"

"No," a voice says from behind me. "It was beautiful."

I turn, slowly, like I'm in a scary movie. My ears are ringing and hot, and my breathing is ragged. I know this voice. It's the worst voice it could possibly be. I look up, from the white tennis shoes to the ripped jeans to the new coat and into the face of the prettiest girl I've ever seen—

Nic.

Chapter 4

This isn't happening.

"I had no idea you could sing, Avery! You sound so good!"

This can't be happening.

"You have to try out for the play! I bet you could play Juliet with a voice like that!"

I'm dying. I'm dying a slow, painful death. This is because I didn't brush my teeth last night. This is because my room is a wreck.

"I'm gonna tell Mrs. Thompson! Hang on, be right back!" Nic rushes off and disappears behind the stage's curtain.

I'm dead.

There's only one thing to do—run. I slam Phantom's closet door closed and grab my backpack and I'm gone, running as fast as I can away from the school and Nic and everything.

I only stop when I'm at the playground near my house, wheezing, my heart tap-dancing against my ribs. Oh man. Oh man, she heard me. I pace in a tight circle, my chest aching. Nic heard me and now she's gonna tell Mrs. Thompson—did she see Phantom? No, definitely not, since Phantom ran away.

Okay. I have to be calm. I sit down on one of the plastic yellow swings and try to breathe. It's hard when there's a hand around your heart, squeezing. Dad says he used to get stressed like I do, but he "grew out of it." I wish I would hurry and grow out of this.

I cradle my head in my hands. I don't know what Nic is going to say to Mrs. Thompson. I can't audition for the play. I've never sung in front of anyone, not for real! Even during the recitals at my old school, I just mouthed the words. I can't do this.

But then again . . . Nic looked so happy. My cheeks burn in my hands. This is bad. All of it. I don't need to see Nic smile, or to sing, or to have friends. I need to think about what I'm going to do, right now. I check my phone—12:24. Lunch is over and I'm a mile down the road.

I call Dad.

He answers after one ring. "Avery?" His voice is high-pitched and scared. "Are you okay?"

"Yes. No. I don't know." I try to take a deep breath, but it's hard to breathe. "I need you to check me out of school."

"Are you sick?" Dad sounds so worried.

"No. I'm just . . . I ran away."

There's a long pause. "From school?"

"Yeah."

"Where are you now?"

I tell him.

Dad sucks in a sharp breath. "Okay. Why are you not at school, Avery?"

I want to tell him about Nic, and what she heard, and that I can't ever see her again because I'll die of embarrassment, but it's no good. My tongue is made of peanut butter and stuck to the roof of my mouth.

"I had to get away," I manage.

"Okay." I can imagine Dad pinching the bridge of his nose. "You're gonna go back to school, and we'll talk about this when I get home tonight. Okay?"

"Okay."

"Text me when you get back. If you don't, I'm coming to get you."

I stand up, my legs wobbly but determined. I shouldn't have called. Dad's really stressed about his new job and Andrew and me, so I need to get it together. I can do this. I'll go back to school and avoid Nic for the rest of my life and everything will be fine. I nod, shouldering my backpack. "Okay. Thanks, Dad."

Everything is not fine.

I avoided Nic in English and we don't have science together, so I thought I was going to be okay. Not even close. As soon as I step into the theater, Nic ambushes me, a huge grin on her face.

"Where'd you go earlier? I came back to get you, and

you weren't there! Come on, we gotta tell Mrs. Thompson!" She grabs my hand and practically drags me to Mrs. Thompson's office. It would be nice to be holding her hand, if mine wasn't so sweaty, and she wasn't dragging me to my certain death.

Mrs. Thompson looks up when we burst in. "What is it, girls?"

"Avery can really sing and you should hear her," Nic says, her words tumbling out like collapsed building blocks. She looks at me, grinning. "Right, Avery? You sound amazing! You could even get the lead part!"

Oh no. No, no, no—

"Is that so?" Mrs. Thompson raises her perfectly mani-cured eyebrows. "What'll you sing for us, Avery?"

I shake my head wildly. Nic laughs. "She's just shy! Come on, Avery, sing the one you were singing earlier."

I look at Nic and her cute freckles and frustrating smile, and I finally say something.

"Why don't you do it?"

Nic blinks at me, and I'm immediately mortified. Not a

word to the prettiest girl in my grade for six months and the *first* thing I say is "Why don't you do it?"?!

My life is over.

Nic recovers and lets out a loud laugh. "I've already tried out! And I can't sing lead anyway. Altos don't lead." It's just for a second, but she looks away from me, her smile fading. Nic is a good actor, the best in our class, in fact. Why wouldn't she be lead?

I don't have time to think about it. Mrs. Thompson clears her throat and looks right at me. "Now, Avery, I'll listen to your audition if you want. But no one can force you. You have to make that decision."

Oh, thank God, I can back out after all. I open my mouth to refuse, but suddenly I'm thinking about Nic's hand in mine and the way Dad sounded worried on the phone and Andrew calling me "pathetic."

I close my mouth.

"Avery?" Mrs. Thompson prompts, one eyebrow raised.

"You'll do it?" Nice asks, her eyes shining with hope.

I look at them both, my chest tight and my breath short.

I should say no. But . . . I really do like to sing. If I get a small part in the choir, I can do my mouthing-the-words trick like I did at my old school and just enjoy practice. And if I do get cast in the play, Dad won't worry. I can also hang out with Phantom more, since I'll be in the theater a lot. And, maybe, I can be friends with Nic. This might just fix everything. I'll get a small part, do the play, and it'll be smooth sailing from there.

I meet Mrs. Thompson's eyes, fighting the fear clutching my lungs, and nod.

"I'll try."

Nic squeals and hugs me, and I'm pretty sure my soul leaves my body.

"Avery, I knew it! You'll be incredible!"

"Okay, okay, girls." Mrs. Thompson laughs. "Nic, you leave and tell the class I'll be a few minutes."

Nic pats me on the back. Her hand is a lot stronger than I'm expecting. "You'll do great!"

And then she's gone, and it's just Mrs. Thompson and me.

"Let's start with a line reading," Mrs. Thompson says. "Do you have your script?"

I nod and fumble with the zipper on my backpack. "Wh-what part should I read?"

"Any," Mrs. Thompson says, smiling.

Okay . . . I pick a smaller part, Juliet's best friend, Amber. Mrs. Thompson reads all the other characters in the section I pick. I'm not great at acting, so when I read it sounds kinda flat. Hopefully it's good enough for a small part.

Mrs. Thompson nods as I finish the second page. "Okay, that's good. Now, for the singing portion."

Sweat beads on my forehead. I know Mrs. Thompson can see it. I clear my throat, suddenly desperate for the bottle of water in my backpack. This was a terrible idea. Even if it will fix everything, can I really do this? Can I really sing in front of her? I tug at my shirt collar, burning up.

"I'm just gonna take my coat off," I tell Mrs. Thompson. She nods, and I shed it like a second skin. I'm still too hot. And light-headed. "I'm gonna get my water bottle, okay?"

"Okay," Mrs. Thompson says.

I drink almost half my water bottle, then immediately want to throw it all up.

"I'm gonna sit down, I think," I tell Mrs. Thompson.

Mrs. Thompson smiles at me, like she's trying to stop herself from laughing. "You don't have to do this if you don't want to, Avery."

"But I want to." That's what I say, but I'm trembling. It's not that I want to; I have to. I think about Dad's worried voice on the phone, and I clench my hands. Now or never, Avery. I can do this.

"Is it okay if I turn around?"

"No. I need to hear you."

I chew on my lip. "Can I close my eyes?"

Mrs. Thompson does her funny smile again. "Sure."

Okay. I can work with that. I touch the YouTube app on my phone and pick the song Nic heard me sing, "Love on Top." I take a shaky breath and press play, then close my eyes.

At first, nothing comes out. I'm just standing there with

my eyes closed, like a huge dummy. But then I get into the beat, feeling it thrum through my ears as it has a million times before. I can't help singing, just a little at first, then louder and louder as the chorus swells, and for just a second, I'm not in Mrs. Thompson's office, I'm in my room, in that tiny closet with Phantom, and I'm free.

The song ends, and the illusion is broken. I open my eyes, and Mrs. Thompson is smiling at me. She claps her hands slowly, still smiling.

"Good job, Miss Williams. I'm proud of you."

My face fills with heat, but it's the good kind for once. Surely I did enough for a small part, way in the back? Surely this will fix everything.

"Thanks, Mrs. Thompson."

Mrs. Thompson ushers me to the door, still smiling. "I'll post the results tomorrow. Good luck."

I leave her office, feeling great. Good luck indeed. This is step one of everything falling into place. It's all gonna work out.

Chapter 5

Nic waves at me frantically as I walk into school the next day. I try to wave back, a painful smile on my face, but before my arm can move, she's right next to me.

"Avery!! I knew you could do it!"

I try to ask her what she's talking about, but she flings her arms around me and suddenly I'm trapped in a tight hug.

Well, maybe asking her can wait.

"I knew it, I just knew it!" Nic squeals in my ear, and we do an awkward, swaying dance. She finally breaks our hug and holds me at arm's length, a huge grin on her face. She searches my expression, her light brown eyes darting back and forth. Heat creeps to the tips of my ears—she's never been this close to me.

But I can't get excited. My uncle Denny told me once that I should never fall in love with a straight girl. It only leads to heartbreak. Denny is the smartest man I know because he lives at home with his mom so he doesn't have to pay rent, so I figure I better listen to him.

"How do you feel?" Nic asks, her hand lingering on my arm. Warmth spreads from her palm to my face. "I knew you'd get the part, I just knew it! Aren't you glad I told Mrs. Thompson you could sing?"

Oh, so this is about the play. I must have gotten a part in the choir! Mrs. Thompson said the results would be up today, but I thought she meant in seventh period, not first thing. I muster the courage to say something. "What did I get?"

Nic blinks at me. "You haven't seen the list yet?"

I shake my head. She pulls up something on her phone and shows it to me. The audition results. Nic is Amber, Juliet's best friend. As expected! It's the second-best part. She has a lot of fun lines. Thomas is Romeo (ugh). And then I see the top of the list.

Oh no.

Oh no.

"Aren't you excited?" Nic says, beaming.

I hear a faint ringing in my ears, but I take a few gulps of air. Nic is wrong. This has to be a mistake. "Stop—stop kidding, Nic. There's no way I'm Juliet."

"Oh, you definitely are," Nic says. "I took a picture of the list this morning. This is so exciting!"

The ringing gets louder. I tug at my sweater, hot, burning. "But it could still . . . it could still be a mistake."

"Are you okay?" Nic says, frowning at me.

I'm not okay. I'm burning up. I can't breathe. It's not a misprint.

I'm really going to be the lead part in the play.

I'm really going to have to *sing* in front of everyone.

"Avery?" Nic's voice is tinged with fear. She grabs my hands, and I hold on for dear life. "Are you okay? What's—"

"I have to go to the nurse." I barely get the words out before I'm wheezing. I bend at the waist, black dots swimming over my vision. The walls are too close, people are staring—

Nic squeezes my hand. "Okay, here we go. Hang on." We stumble to the nurse's office, me focusing on breathing and not passing out and making a fool of myself.

Nurse Biles meets me at the door. She's a bigger lady, and she always wears super-glamorous makeup. Not that I can see it right now. I'm on the edge of fainting.

"Oh, Avery," Nurse Biles says, clicking her tongue. "I thought we were getting better."

"C-can you help?" Nic's voice is small and scared. Her fingernails dig into my skin. "I think she's dying. Should we call 911?"

"She's not dying." Nurse Biles guides me to a familiar cot. She gets to her knees in front of me. "Okay, Avery, look at me. Just like last time."

I nod, my throat too constricted to speak.

"Tell me three things you can see."

At first, it's hard to think about anything except the play and singing in front of everyone and Nic staring at me with a look of horror. But Nurse Biles is waiting on me, so I force myself to look around the room.

"Coat." I take a gulp of air. "Your watch. Umm, my shoes."

"Good!" Mrs. Biles smiles at me encouragingly. "What about your new shoes? Tell me about them."

"They're not new. But I washed them over the break. So they'd look new."

"Well, you did a good job. They're still so white."

My chest swells with pride and, with it, precious air. "Yeah, it's really hard to do! But Dad says I can get new ones next year if I keep these clean."

"I know you can do it." Nurse Biles pats my knee, her big eyes soft. "How do you feel now?"

I take a while to answer. My hands are shaking now, and I'm still panting, but at least I can breathe a little. I sneak a glance at Nic, and a piece of me dies—she's looking at me like I'm a ghost. Or a monster.

Nurse Biles follows my gaze. "Ah, Miss Pearson, time to go! Thank you for helping Avery here."

Nic protests, but Nurse Biles ushers her out of the room and closes the door. She stands by the door, her hands behind her back.

"Okay, how are you feeling now? It's just you and me."

I shrug. The panic is gone, but shame is creeping into my chest. This first started happening last year, when Dad said we were moving. All of a sudden, I couldn't breathe and I almost passed out. Dad took me to the hospital because we thought I was dying. The doctor told me it was a panic attack, and I should try to not stress out so much. Easy for him to say. Since then, I've had fourteen—fifteen, now—panic attacks. I know what to do now, and how to calm down. But I've never had one in front of someone who isn't Dad or Nurse Biles.

I've never had one in front of someone I like.

"Avery?"

"I'm okay." I take a deep breath to prove it. I'm still shaking, but it's over. I hope.

"Good." Nurse Biles sits on the cot next to me. "What brought it on?"

I explain the play to her, and how I'm in the lead role now. Nurse Biles nods slowly.

"It sounds like it'll put a lot of stress on you. Are you sure you can do it?"

I look down at my tennis shoes. I don't know. This is really bad. Juliet has a ton of lines. And a lot of singing too.

"Just think about it. Don't do it if it's going to hurt you. Your health is more important than a play." Nurse Biles sits at her desk. "Now, Avery, you know I have to call your dad."

A fresh wave of panic hits me. "Please don't! I feel better—"

"He made me promise to call him if it happened again." Nurse Biles seems apologetic. "Sorry, Avery."

I lean back against the cot, defeated. How is this for not worrying Dad? He's gonna freak out. I close my eyes and wish I'd never auditioned for the play. I wish I'd never sung out loud at all.

So much for everything working out.

Chapter 6

When I see Dad, I almost burst into tears.

His face is panicked, and he's breathing hard, like he ran all the way here. He doesn't say anything at first—he just gives me a big hug. I really do start crying then, but just a little, so he won't see.

Dad breaks our hug after a while and puts his heavy hands on my shoulders. "Are you okay?"

"I'm okay." I wipe my eyes, trying to hold in my tears. "I promise. You can go back to work, I swear."

"No. You're still shaking, Avery."

"Only a little. I'm okay, I promise."

Dad glances at Nurse Biles behind us. Then he meets my

eyes, his brow creased with worry. "How about a compromise? I took half a day off anyway, so we'll get lunch, and I'll bring you back for your last three classes. Deal?"

If he's already taken off . . . And I don't really want to go to math anyway. I nod, and Dad hugs me again. "Okay, let's go. We'll be back before you know it."

Dad stops by the front office and talks with the receptionist. The halls are empty—everyone is in class. Thank God. I wipe my face again nervously. I don't know if anyone can tell if I've been crying.

Dad walks close to me as we leave the school. His car is parked right at the front. "This is the fire lane," I tell him as he unlocks the doors with the key fob. "You're gonna get a ticket."

"Cut me some slack," Dad says, smiling. He jogs ahead of me and opens the passenger-side door. "Hey, you can sit up front today."

Uh oh. I must look awful. Dad never lets me sit up front, unless something bad happens. I got to sit up front when my goldfish died, when Andrew's friends broke my favorite doll, and when Dad first told me we were moving. And now.

I don't say anything as I climb into the passenger seat. Dad makes sure I'm buckled up, then climbs into the driver's side.

I wait for Dad to say something, but he doesn't. He just drives around for a little while, and then down a long road that eventually leads to an old, run-down house that looks haunted. We got lost on that road when we first moved. Everyone laughed and said it's a rookie mistake—it's a road to nowhere.

"So," Dad finally says. "What brought it on?"

I look out the window as we pass some cows. They're all just standing there, chewing grass. Lying down. Mooing, I guess. I bet cows don't get nervous about mooing to one another.

"Avery?"

I heave a sigh. "I got a part in the play."

"Oh yeah? But that's a good thing, isn't it?"

"I got *the* part, Dad. The lead. I have to play Juliet."

"Avery!" I glance at Dad, and he's grinning, his smile lighting up his whole face. "Congratulations! I knew you could do it. You have such a lovely voice, and now you get to share it with everyone!"

"Yeah," I say, gripping my knees with sweaty palms. "Everyone."

Dad's smile fades. "You're pretty nervous, huh?"

Nervous doesn't begin to cover it, but I nod.

"It's okay to be nervous. Completely normal, in fact. But you'll have time to practice beforehand. When's the play again?"

"Valentine's Day."

"Oh yeah, plenty of time. Six weeks. It'll be great, Avery. You'll make some friends, and you'll get to sing—I think this can be really good for you."

I stare out the window again. I just wanted a small part in the choir. I didn't want this. How can I play the lead part in a play if I've never done it before? How can I sing in front of an auditorium full of people? But Dad looks *so* happy.

Dad pauses for a moment as he slows to a stop for a red light. "Not excited, huh?"

"It's not that." I keep my eyes on the window. "I just wanted a little part, but now I have to play Juliet and I don't want to because I've never had a lead part before and what if I can't sing in front of everybody?" I have to stop because my chest feels tight. I close my eyes and try to breathe deeply.

"I understand." I open my eyes, and Dad's looking at me, his eyes soft. "I know you're scared, but I also know you'll do an amazing job. And I'll take off from work to see you! Six weeks is plenty of notice."

Tears well up in my eyes, but I wipe them away before he can see. I can't back out now. It's too late. If Dad is taking off from work to see me, I have to do this. I have to make sure Dad thinks I'm fine so he doesn't worry. I can't make his life harder than it already is.

"It's okay," I say, taking a deep breath. I think of Nic's arms around me this morning in her excitement. I imagine acting with her every day after school. "I can do the play."

Dad grins at me and pats my arm. "Attagirl. But you can stop at any time, you know."

I nod, but dread sinks to the bottom of my stomach. I can't stop now. I have the lead part in *Romeo and Juliet*. I just have to deal with it.

Chapter 7

Dad and I go home, and I nap, and then he takes me to McDonald's for lunch. I don't go back to school until fifth period, when the day is almost over. I wish I could have taken the whole day off, but I need to hear what Mrs. Thompson has to say about practice.

I struggle through fifth and sixth period, and then it's time for theater. I stand outside, palms sweaty, and try to control my breathing. I can do this. Just one more period, and I can go home. One more. Come on, Avery. No fear.

I walk into theater, and a few people turn to look at me. My face gets warm, then hot as I spot Nic staring at me. The heat dies when she quickly looks down at her lap.

This is the worst day of my life. I had a panic attack, and

now Nic thinks I'm an even bigger weirdo than before. She can't even look at me. And now all the other kids in my class are staring at me and in six weeks everyone will be staring at me—

"Miss Williams?" Mrs. Thompson's voice snaps me out of my spiral. Everyone's sitting at the foot of the stage. "Come on, sit, so we can get started."

I wipe my sweaty hands on my jeans and sit at the back. But now Emily and Sarah are watching me, whispering to each other. I wish I could disappear.

"I'm sure everyone saw the cast list. Congratulations to our actors and crew! Especially our newcomer—"

Please don't say my name, please don't say my name, please—

"—Avery Williams as Juliet!"

That's it. I'm running away from home. I'm never coming back here. Andrew's just gonna have to homeschool me.

Everyone looks back at me. Everyone except Nic, who's staring at her script like it has the secrets of the universe. I sink lower in my chair, the edges of a panic attack fluttering in my stomach.

"We'll start practice immediately. We'll do a quick run-through of the script now. Hurry, don't just sit there!"

I fumble with my backpack and withdraw the script. I stare forlornly at all my meticulous notes about the back-drops and set design. Useless.

Emily is the narrator. She starts speaking, her voice loud and confident. ". . . this is *not* a tale of woe, between Juliet and her Romeo."

My turn. My mouth is a desert. I take a shaky breath and speak. "Making deliveries for M-Mom and Dad is so annoying—"

"Speak up!" Thomas complains. "I can barely hear you."

My hands are shaking. I can't do this. Maybe Dad will let me change schools—

"Avery?" Mrs. Thompson prompts. "It's okay, keep read-ing. Don't worry about volume for now."

Deep breaths. I restart and somehow muddle my way

through the rest of the scene. Thank goodness we don't have to sing yet.

The bell rings in the middle of act 2. Everyone starts grabbing their backpacks while Mrs. Thompson yells for us to practice at home. I stuff my script into my bag, my legs trembling with relief. I survived today. Just six more weeks.

"I can't believe she got Juliet."

I freeze, not looking up from my bag. I can't tell who's talking.

"Right?" someone else whispers. "She's terrible."

I stay bent over my backpack until everyone is gone, the weight of the words freezing me in place. It's true. I'm terrible. And if I don't figure out how to get better, everyone will know it.

Chapter 8

"It's not fair," I whine to Phantom. Dad's gonna be late again, extra late because he has to make up for the hours he wasted with me, so I'm hanging out with Phantom. I came straight to her closet as soon as everyone else had left the theater. She's ignoring me though and wolfing down the cheeseburger I brought her.

"At least one of us is happy," I grumble as she licks cheese from the McDonald's wrapper. Wait, can cats even eat cheese? Maybe, since cats drink milk? But I think I read online that milk isn't good for cats. I frown at her as she starts batting around the wrapper, her tail twitching. I need to learn more about cats.

"Do you think I can be a good Juliet?"

Phantom slaps the wrapper into the closet, then gets bored and starts cleaning her whiskers. Not a promising response.

"I know I'm new at acting. But surely I can do enough to not embarrass myself? In front of the whole school? And Dad?"

Oh man. If Dad really does take off from work to see the play, I can't let him see me pass out from fear. My stomach clenches, and I can taste the chicken nuggets I had for lunch at the top of my throat.

The next thing I know, Phantom settles her heavy weight on my chest, her eyes half closed, purring. I put a hand on her back, my fingers sinking into her soft fur. Slowly, as I stroke her back, the panic fades and I'm calmer.

"Phantom," I say, my eyes on the dark ceiling. "Maybe it won't be so bad after all. I can visit you more now. And I won't be alone at the house all the time. Maybe it's a good thing."

Phantom yawns in response and hops off my chest. She goes to her cat bed and flops down, staring pointedly at me. Time for a nap, I guess.

I say goodbye to Phantom and close her closet door. I check my phone as I descend the steps on the stage. Four thirty. Dad won't be home yet, and the buses have left already, so I'll walk home. Not a big deal, but I wish it wasn't so cold—

I notice something out of the corner of my eye. I look up, frozen, into the surprised face of Harper, who's sitting at the edge of the stage.

"Oh, whoa, I didn't know anyone was still here." Harper's voice is soft, deeper than I imagined. I've never talked to her before. What's she doing in the theater? Wait, did she hear me talking to Phantom? No, she looks just as surprised as I am. So Phantom's safe for now—

Harper raises her eyebrows at me, and my palms get sweaty. She wants me to answer her, but my throat closes up, refusing to let a word out. I could say *How are you?* Or *I like your play* or *Wow, sure is wild how they cast a girl to sing when she can't even speak normally, huh?* No, that last one is really depressing. I fight to keep control of my breathing as Harper's expression changes into curiosity.

"I'm Harper. Who're you?"

Her tone is a little abrasive, but her expression is curious, not threatening. I try to say my name, but my throat won't let me. I swallow the last bit of spit in my mouth, but that doesn't help.

"So it's true you don't talk, huh." Harper nods to herself, seemingly deep in thought. "I heard you're playing Juliet. No offense, but you're not how I imagined her at all."

A twinge of annoyance interrupts my building panic. This happened a lot at my old school too. *Sorry, girls without straight hair and perfect teeth can't play lead roles.* Well, why the heck not? "Is it 'cause I'm Black?"

Harper's eyes widen, and my hands shoot to my mouth. I said that out loud. I said that out loud!! God, if you're real, you can take me right now.

"No, no, I didn't mean that!" Harper's turning a deep shade of red now. My face is just as hot as hers looks. "I just meant I pictured her as a lot taller and stuff. I didn't mean, umm, white."

It's not like I care, not really. It's too late—I have the

part, and I guess she'll have to deal with a short Black Juliet. Who can't talk.

"Well, now I've made it really awkward," Harper says, laughing a little. She fidgets, twisting the tail of her shirt in her hands. I remember her terrified expression when Mrs. Thompson was introducing her and some of the fear fades. She gets nervous sometimes too.

I take a deep breath. I can do this. Just one sentence. I try to remember when I wasn't anxious, when Phantom was purring on my chest. I hang on to that feeling like a lifeline.

"It's okay." I give her a wobbly smile. "I'm Avery. And I can talk, I just—I get nervous sometimes."

Harper's face lights up, and some of her blush disappears. "I get nervous too. I almost died when Mrs. Thompson made me stand in front of everyone."

"I know." Wait, is that a bad thing to say? Sweat prickles at the edge of my hairline.

Harper laughs, making me jump. "That obvious, huh?" She looks down at her shoes, her smile fading. They're red Converse, but they're dirty and old, like the ones I used to wear before we moved here. "It's hard when everyone's staring at you. That's why I write the plays instead of acting them out."

Yeah, if only I could be in Harper's position. But I'm not good at English or creative writing, so maybe not. I open my mouth to say something else, but my phone buzzes. I pull it out—a text from Dad.

On my way home! We'll get that ice cream like I promised.

"I have to go," I tell Harper. "Dad'll be mad if I'm not home when he gets back."

"Oh yeah, it's kinda late." Harper hesitates, like she wants to say something else but changes her mind.

It is kinda late . . . Why isn't Harper going home yet? Technically, we're not supposed to be in the school past four, but no one checks the theater. Wait, how does Harper know that? She's not in theater—she's in creative writing. What's she doing here?

I want to ask, but Harper waves at me, one hand in her pocket. "See you later, Avery. Maybe tomorrow?"

"Yeah," I say, smiling tentatively. "Maybe tomorrow."

Chapter 9

I stare at my script, willing myself to memorize the lines.

It's almost bedtime, and I've done everything except practice. I did my homework, watched a makeup tutorial, practiced the makeup tutorial on myself (and quickly wiped my face off because Dad would die if he knew I was putting on makeup), played a Pokémon game, and it's still just nine o'clock. I've run out of things to do. I have to practice now.

"Okay, Avery," I say out loud, flipping to the first song. I have the YouTube link Mrs. Thompson sent us at the ready. "One song. How hard can it be?"

I hold my breath and listen to the song. Mrs. Thompson is singing, surprisingly. I also hear two more voices, but I don't know who they are. I just focus on Mrs. Thompson's, because she's a soprano and that's what Juliet is too. The lyrics are kind of goofy but not terrible. The harmonies are really nice. I listen four times, my foot tapping to the beat, and on the fifth, I start singing. It's a little rough but not awful. Also not good enough for anyone else to hear me though.

"Hey!"

I take off my headphones, heart pounding. Andrew's standing in my doorway, glaring at me.

"What the heck are you singing? Sounds like a dying duck up here."

"Go away," I growl. I put my headphones back on. "Get out of my room."

Andrew doesn't leave. To my horror, he comes to my desk and looks over my shoulder. "What's this for? A play?"

Maybe if I just answer his questions, he'll leave me alone. "Yes. I got a part."

"Like a speaking part? Not the crew?"

"Yep."

"Oh God, so I gotta hear this for six months?"

"Six weeks." I grab my script and turn away from him. "Now I have to practice. Go away."

"Why'd you try out? I thought you hated singing in front of people."

What is Andrew's deal today? He's not even on his phone. "What do you want?"

"Nothing. Just curious," Andrew says. "I just know how you can get when you're stressed. I don't wanna deal with it."

Man, what a jerk. I sit up straighter and take my headphones off. "Dad says I can do it."

"Yeah, well." Andrew finally moves to the door, thank goodness. "Dad's an optimist. I'm realistic." He puts his hands in his pockets but doesn't leave. He looks deep in thought.

"What now?" I finally ask.

He looks at me. I'm surprised when he's not smiling. "Don't do it for Dad. Do it for you."

What's that supposed to mean? I've already tried out. It's too late. "Okay?"

Andrew waves and leaves. Without closing my door. Ugh.

I slump against my desk chair. I don't get Andrew sometimes. Before we moved, he was a nice brother. We played Pokémon together (even though he never let me win). He'd take me to the movies. But since the move, he's been awful. And now what's this? Giving me advice? Andrew doesn't know anything about theater. He played basketball at his old school. Maybe that's part of what's wrong. He's not playing basketball now and has too much time to annoy me.

I practice a little more, until I'm satisfied I know Juliet's part on the first song. I climb into bed, but right before I fall asleep, I remember what Andrew said. *Don't do it for Dad. Do it for you.* But why? Dad was really excited. I can get excited about it too, after more practice maybe. It's a long time before I fall asleep, but I take it as a good sign the song is stuck in my head until I do.

Chapter 10

"With more feeling, Miss Williams," Mrs. Thompson scolds me on our third run-through of the script. I'm supposed to be saying a line about how hard it is to love the rival donut shop's donuts more than the ones your parents make, but I'm almost at my limit. Everyone is staring at me. My armpits are a sweaty pool. I want to go home. I'm about to faint.

The bell rings, mercifully, and everyone starts packing up their bags. I sink into my chair, breathing raggedly. My script is damp from my palms. This isn't working.

It's been a couple of days since I got the part and my whole life fell apart. I've been getting better at reading my part in class, but when I look up and see them watching me,

I get freaked out. I hope I can fix this before Valentine's Day, because otherwise this play is gonna suck. And what's worse is that Nic hasn't looked at me in two days. She probably wants nothing to do with me since she saw me freak out. It figures—I get a terrible part in the play, I have a panic attack that makes Dad worry, *and* my crush thinks I'm disgusting. The trifecta of suckiness. Maybe I'm cursed. Maybe I kicked puppies in a past life and this is my punishment.

I wait for everyone to leave before visiting Phantom. I play with her for a while—I wish I could get her cat toys, but she seems happy enough batting around bits of paper with me—but the whole time I'm listening for Harper. I haven't seen her since we talked, and I'm kinda disappointed. She seemed cool, and maybe we could be friends. Maybe. If I don't have a panic attack around her, I guess. Which I have a bad track record for so far.

I wait until four thirty, but Harper doesn't come, so I close Phantom's door and head home. It's getting dark already.

Dad would kill me if he knew I wasn't home. Lucky for me that Andrew isn't home either, so he can't snitch on me.

I'm passing the park by my house when I hear someone call my name. I turn in surprise, and my stomach does a funny flip—it's Nic. She's running toward me, out of breath. I shuffle my feet uncertainly. What does she want? I thought she didn't want anything to do with me anymore . . .

Nic catches up to me, panting. She meets my eyes, and I'm even more surprised to see she's almost crying.

"Hey, Avery." She takes a shaky breath and stands up taller. Her expression is focused and solemn. "I'm sorry for what I did. I'm really sorry."

I blink at her uncertainly. "Umm . . . what did you do?"

Nic's resolve crumbles, and she looks confused. "I made you have that breakdown, remember? It's all my fault. I thought you knew about the results, but you didn't, and I made you go through something awful. I've been trying to talk to you, but I thought you might be mad. But I had to apologize."

I stare at her for a full three seconds before a laugh bubbles out of me. "Nic, that's not how it works. At all."

Nic searches my face anxiously. "What do you mean?"

"You didn't make me have a panic attack." I wipe my eyes, still grinning. "It's more of a . . . me thing."

"I still don't understand. I told you about getting the part, and then . . ."

"Sometimes I get really stressed out," I explain. "And my body freaks out. It's not your fault."

"Oh." Nic's face crumples with relief. "I'm so glad. I mean, I'm glad that it wasn't my fault. I felt terrible. I haven't slept in two days, you know."

The last of my laughter is gone, and suddenly I'm aware that I'm talking to Nic again, all alone, in front of a park. Heat fills my face, and I inch toward home. "Umm, well, I should go—"

"Wait! Is that why you can't talk sometimes? Because you're stressed?"

Oh man, hitting me with the hard questions. It's getting

dark and I'm starting to feel sweaty and light-headed. "I—I have to go! Bye!"

Nic says something, but I take off running. I run all the way home, up my steps, and into my room. I'm panting, my lungs restricting, but I'm grinning. *Nic Pearson* talked to me! And I didn't pass out! And she doesn't hate me! I grab my pillow and scream into it, dancing in a circle. I did it. I talked to Harper and Nic in one week. Maybe I'm getting better!

Maybe Nic and I can be friends after all.

"So, do you like him?" Nic says, her tone playful.

"Yeah," I say, my eyes glued to my script. "I like him a lot."

"He is pretty cute," Nic continues. I look up from my script, and she's smiling at me. "Eleven out of ten."

Why am I so hot all of a sudden? We're just reading our parts for the play. She's Juliet's best friend, and I'm Juliet. I gotta focus. "There's no point in having a scale if you're just gonna break it."

"Don't be so uptight!" Nic laughs and I swear my heart is beating triple time. She has dimples. I never noticed until now. She leans closer, even though we're sitting across the room from each other. "So, have you kissed him yet?"

The bell rings, and thank God because I am *definitely* not thinking about kissing Romeo.

"Good job today!" Mrs. Thompson yells over everyone packing up. "We'll start the singing rehearsals soon! Make sure you're practicing!"

Oh boy. And just like that, my good mood's gone. But it's not all bad; Nic gets her backpack and waves at me as she leaves. I try to wave too, but my hand is glued to my side. I hope she sees me smiling.

I put my sweaty script away, but I notice someone out of the corner of my eye. It's Emily and another girl from our class, Haley. They're talking with Thomas.

"She's doing okay now," Emily says, her voice hushed. I strain to hear her, putting my script away extra slow.

"She's only good with Nic's parts," Thomas says. "She sucks with mine."

My stomach drops. They're talking about me.

"That's 'cause you're so dry," Haley teases him, elbowing him in the side. He doesn't smile back at her.

"I just think you should be qualified to get the leading role in a play. I mean, she was in the crew last time. How is she gonna do a lead part?"

Emily glances at me, and we meet each other's eyes. I hope she can't see mine are full of tears.

"Uh, let's go, guys." Emily ushers Thomas and Haley out of the theater, and I'm the only one left. Even Mrs. Thompson is gone. I run to the back of the theater, already crying.

I reach Phantom's closet in record time. Phantom meows and circles my legs while I wipe my eyes.

"It's not fair," I choke out, my breathing ragged. "I'm trying. I'm practicing. Why is it so hard for me?"

Phantom puts her front paws on my leg and meows again. I pick her up and hug her to my chest. She purrs and licks my tears away. Eventually, my breathing calms, and soon I'm just sniffling. I bury my face in Phantom's fur.

"At least you don't care about plays. You probably don't even care about Romeo and Juliet. It's a dumb story anyway."

"Yeah, I agree."

I turn in shock. Harper's standing right behind me, grinning sheepishly. "I heard you crying, so I— Holy cow, is that a cat?"

Chapter 11

I'm too shocked to really feel the panic at first. All my brain can do is go over the facts. Harper is here. She heard me crying. She saw Phantom. Well, she's seeing Phantom right now, because she's cooing and holding out her hand for Phantom to sniff. Phantom does cautiously, then rubs her head against Harper's hand, purring.

That snaps me out of it. I back away, holding Phantom like a lifeline. "Wh-what're you doing here?"

Harper frowns. "I heard you crying, remember? Whose cat is this?"

I'm finding it hard to breathe again. I didn't think about what would happen if anyone found Phantom . . .

Will Harper tell? Will Mrs. Thompson take her away? What if Phantom won't come back anymore and then I'll have exactly zero friends? But wait, I need to calm down. Phantom is calm, still purring. She's not too worried about it. I gulp in some air. "I—I found her here. She's my cat. Sorta."

"You found her in the theater?" I nod and point at the closet. Harper opens the door, and her eyes widen. "Oh wow! This is so cool. I love cats, but my mom said we can't have any pets. Can I hold her?"

I want to say no, but I know that's not cool. Phantom must like her, because she usually runs when she hears someone coming. I hold her out to Harper, and Harper scoops her from my arms and cradles her against her chest. She grins at me. "Oh my God, she's so cute. What'd you name her?"

"Phantom. Like *Phantom of the Opera*. 'Cause she lives in a theater." I'm talking too much. I shut my mouth as Harper pets her.

"Did you buy all this stuff for her?" Harper asks, nodding

at Phantom's bed and bowls. I nod, and Harper examines the cat stuff, saying "Wow" and "This is so cool." She's pretty excited, which helps me calm down a little. It's kinda cool that someone else knows now.

After a while, she puts Phantom down, and Phantom flops onto her bed.

"She's pretty fat for a stray," Harper says, folding her arms. That's what I said! "Do you think she belongs to someone?"

Yeah, me. But no, I guess I never thought about that . . . Maybe someone's missing Phantom. My chest constricts at the idea of somebody coming to claim her. "I don't know, maybe?"

"We should look for her owner," Harper says. She grins at me. "If we don't find anyone, you can keep her!"

I shake my head. "I can't. My brother's allergic."

"Oh, that sucks." Harper's face falls. There's a long silence, like she's waiting for me to say something. But what? We stare at each other for a few more uncomfortable seconds. Finally, Harper says, "Do you want to look for her owner anyway?"

Oh! Warmth fills my face. She wants to hang out with me? Even though I'm so weird? And I mean, if we do find Phantom's owners, that's better for Phantom. It has to be lonely in the theater. Even though then I'd be the lonely one.

"Okay." I smile at Harper. "I'm in."

"Awesome!"

"But it has to be a secret. We can't tell anyone." If we tell Mrs. Thompson, or even someone else in theater, they might take her away from us. I want to find Phantom's owners, if she has any, but I want to spend as much time with her as I can. I get a pang of sadness when I think of her leaving the closet. And me.

"Definitely. Our secret." Harper grins back at me. "This'll be fun! It's late now, but maybe we can start looking Wednesday after school?"

"Like . . . online?"

"Yeah! I don't have a smartphone, so we can use the library."

I nod, a little overwhelmed. I was scared Harper would tell on me, but she's pretty cool. And we'll get to hang out after school. I don't want to jinx it, but this is almost like . . . what friends do.

Chapter 12

The next day, I walk to the park after school, deep in thought.

I'm in a weird place. Nic talked to me yesterday, smiled at me in class. Then Harper invited me to go somewhere after school. She stopped me today in math and said she was excited to look for Phantom's owner with me. I'm a little confused. I haven't really said much to Harper or Nic, but they're being really nice to me. I don't want to get my hopes up though. This has happened before, and it didn't go well.

I sit down on one of the swings and check my phone. I scroll through my texts, all the way until almost a year ago. I stop at Layla's name, but I don't touch it. I miss her sometimes, but she hasn't texted me in a long time. At first, we would text at least every two days, sending each other memes and cat pictures. But then she joined the swim team and it was once a week, then once a month. Even after I told her happy birthday, she waited a week to answer and it was just a "thanks." I stopped texting her after that. Dad says when someone shows you how they feel, believe them. I do believe her. But I don't know how that translates to Nic and Harper. Maybe they want to be friends, but maybe they just think the girl who can't talk is weird and they're curious.

I put my phone away and draw a circle in the sand at my feet with one toe. I wish I could talk to someone, even Phantom, but she wasn't in her bed after school. Cats have busy lives, I guess. Busier than mine.

"Avery? Is that you?"

I look up in alarm. Nic's voice—there she is, by the fence. She waves at me, and before I can wave back, she comes into the park. I scramble to my feet, my heart pounding. What does she want?

"What's up?" Nic asks, like we've been friends forever.

Like she's not the prettiest girl in school. "Do you walk this way to go home?"

I try to answer, but my tongue is glued to the roof of my mouth. I manage to nod.

"Oh, cool!" Nic doesn't seem bothered by my silence. "I come here a lot because of the dog park! Well, when it's my turn to walk her. Which is all the time since Eric is so lazy."

Walk her? Eric? I can't keep up with the conversation. I want to ask for clarity, but my throat is tight. Not yet.

"So, umm, I think you're doing really well in class," Nic says. She's still smiling, but she looks a little uncomfortable. I've gotta say something, quick. "What do you think about the songs?"

I struggle to find words for a second, but I get distracted when a huge dog gallops to the edge of the open park gate. There's a dog park next to the regular park, but honestly this is the first time I've seen a dog in there. Nic pats her leg, and the dog lopes to her side, tongue hanging out.

All my panic is gone in an instant. I love cats, but I really like dogs too. I hold on to the edge of my pants, aching to pet it. It's got curly tan fur and golden eyes and it's so cute! I wish every day Andrew wasn't allergic.

"Do you want to pet her?" Nic asks.

Nic is an angel. I owe her my life.

My tongue finally unsticks itself from the roof of my mouth. "Yeah, thanks!" I bend to pet the dog, and she runs to me. Her fur is so soft, and she's so cute. "Is she your dog?"

"Yep! Her name's Noodle."

"Noodle? Are you serious?" When Nic nods, I grin and rub behind the dog's ears. "That's the best name I've ever heard. Is she a goldendoodle or a labradoodle? I like both, but goldendoodles have a better temperament, I think. I don't have a dog, and I really want one, but my brother, Andrew, is allergic. Isn't that awful? He's a jerk and he has allergies, so I can't even get a pet to talk to. And it sucks because Dad's working all the time, so it's just me in that big empty house with no one to talk to ever."

Nic stares down at me as Noodle rolls onto her back for a belly rub. She's quiet for a second, then says, "Avery, that's the most I've ever heard you say."

Heat immediately fills my face. I scramble to my feet and back away, even though Noodle whines and nudges my hand. "Oh, umm, sorry."

"No, this is great!" Nic's smiling, and her freckles are so adorable in the low lighting. "You like dogs, right? Maybe Noodle can help you."

"What do you mean?"

"You're having trouble reading your part in class, right? Well, just the parts with Thomas, but he's terrible so that's expected. Anyway, what if we practice with Noodle?"

"Uh . . ."

"You'll read your part to me, maybe while Noodle is there, and eventually you won't be scared to do it for real!"

This is definitely not gonna work.

"I see you're doubting my plan." Nic stands up tall, her chin elevated. With her hands on her hips, she looks like a superhero. "Trust me, Avery. We'll make you the perfect Juliet."

"Okay," I say slowly. It sounds like a terrible idea, but I think about Emily, Haley, and Thomas making fun of me and wince. It's worth a try. I don't want to ruin everyone's play. And Noodle is really cute . . . "But when will we practice? You can't bring Noodle to school."

"Oh, you can come to my house." My jaw must be on the floor, because Nic looks away, laughing. "Only if you want to!"

Come over to Nic's house. The prettiest girl in school. Me. *And* I get to play with her dog? This has to be a trick. This can't be real.

Nic is waiting on me, so I blurt out, "I'll have to ask my dad." It's true (he'd never let me go to someone's house without me asking), but I hate that Nic's face falls a little.

"Okay! Just let me know." She clips Noodle's leash to her collar and waves. "See you tomorrow, Avery!"

I wave too, a funny feeling in my gut. I talked to Nic, a little, and I didn't pass out. And I talked to Harper too. Maybe this play is a good thing. Well, I wouldn't go that far. But things are kinda looking up.

Chapter 13

I push around the last bit of spaghetti on my plate, trying to figure out how to ask Dad to let me go to Nic's house.

There's a trick to asking Dad about these things. Ever since The Incident (Andrew got invited to a birthday party and the other kids teased him until he cried to come home), Dad is really paranoid about us going to places he doesn't know. It hasn't mattered to me because I don't really go anywhere, but he and Andrew are always fighting about where Andrew's going.

"What's wrong?" Dad asks me as he returns from the kitchen. His plate is piled high with spaghetti. Dad's eyebrows furrow. "Did you have another panic attack?"

"No," I assure him. I make a heart out of my leftover noodles while I pick my words. "So, Dad . . ."

"No."

"Dad! I haven't even asked!"

"Okay, okay," he says, laughing. "Go on."

"What if I wanted to, umm, go to a friend's house."

Andrew looks up from his phone for the first time all night. "I thought you didn't have friends."

I shoot him a dirty look before looking at Dad again. "It's just for a little while. To practice for the play."

Dad pauses mid-twirl and narrows his eyes. Uh oh. Not a good sign.

"Who is this friend?"

"Her name is Nic. She plays Juliet's best friend in the play. She's really cool, I promise."

"Where does she live?"

"Around here! We ride the bus together."

"Who are her parents?"

I bite my bottom lip. I don't know. I never asked.

Dad crosses his arms, seemingly deep in thought. "I'm not sure about this, Avery. You've never mentioned her before. And now you want to go to her house?"

"Let her go," Andrew says, surprising me. "She's been miserable for months. It's depressing."

I guess Dad is surprised too, because he doesn't say anything for a few seconds. Then he looks at me and shrugs, smiling a little. "Okay, you can go. But—I have to meet her parents first. Do you have their number?"

"I can get it," I say, pulling out my phone. I have Nic's number because we have a cast group chat, but I've never texted her before. I take a deep breath and send a text before I can chicken out.

Hey Nic its Avery. Dad wants to meet ur parents before I can come over

The text bubble pops up immediately.

YES!! Hang on let me ask

I wait, knots in my stomach. Dad's talking to Andrew about college, so at least they're not staring at me while I wait. Three long minutes tick by before the bubble pops up again.

Mom says that's cool! Can you and your dad come over Friday?? Around 7?

I touch the collar of my shirt, already sweaty. This is way more than I bargained for. But when I ask Dad, he nods, and I text Nic back, panic and fear and something a lot like excitement swimming in my chest.

We'll be there.

After school on Wednesday, I go to the library to wait on Harper.

I'm starting to get that nervous, sweaty feeling I got when I tried to talk to Nic on the first day of the semester. I adjust my backpack, then walk in a circle, then rub my damp hands on my jeans. I can do this. I just have to be normal. Not a big deal. Everyone else does it. Except me.

"Hey, Avery."

I look up, heart hammering, and Harper's standing just

a few feet from me. I didn't see her coming. How does she do that? I didn't hear her coming when she saw me with Phantom either.

I try to talk, but Harper's standing there, just waiting, and my tongue freezes up. I manage a nod though, and she smiles at me.

"Ready to get searchin'?"

I nod again, trying to swallow the lump in my throat, and Harper pushes open the door to the library. There's hardly anyone in here—just one librarian I've never met, because I don't come here very much. At my old school I would hang out in the library at lunch, but now I have the theater.

"Hi, Mrs. Carter," Harper says to the librarian. "How are you?"

"Doing great," the librarian says, smiling at Harper. She's a tall lady with short black hair. "What're you getting today? We have some new fantasy titles in."

Harper looks interested, but she shakes her head. "Nothing. Avery and I want to use a computer for a few minutes. Can we, even though it's after school?"

The librarian smiles at her. "Sure, go ahead."

"Thanks, Mrs. Carter!" Harper says goodbye and leads me to the computers. She must be good friends with the librarian, because there's a big sign over the section that says COMPUTER HOURS: 8:00 A.M.–3:00 P.M. and it's already three thirty. Does she read a lot? Well, she has to, since she wrote a whole play. It probably counts as practice, like singing a song over and over until you know all the notes. Maybe I should read more.

Harper turns on the computer and types in her library card number from memory. I don't even know where my library card is. "Where should we start?" Harper asks me.

I take a deep breath. I can do this. "Maybe . . . the shelters and vet clinics? But I don't know which ones are close, because I just moved here. Which you know already." I shut up before I make things worse.

Harper smiles at me. "I did know. Where'd you go before?"

I fidget a little. This is an easy question, but I still feel a little panicked. "I—I went to Eufaula Middle. That's the name of the city."

"Oh yeah?" To my slight horror, Harper pulls up Google and types in "ufalla." Luckily, Google corrects her, so I don't have to. "Oh wow, that's a long way from here! Like four hours."

Yeah, almost exactly four hours. Riding in the car with Andrew that long was torture. He was still really mad that Dad made us move right before his senior year, so he didn't talk the whole time. Dad kept trying to start a conversation, but Andrew wouldn't answer. It was miserable.

I watch Harper google three vet clinics and two animal shelters, pulling up the lost pet ads from each place, but no Phantom. There is one cat that sort of looks like her, but it's too skinny and has a notch in one ear. There's a bunch of really cute cats missing in Cullman, Alabama, but none are Phantom.

Harper leans back in her chair and sighs. "A strikeout. I guess we could look in other cities, but how far can a cat go?"

I shrug, trying to hide my relief. We didn't find her, so maybe she really is a stray. A stray that eats a lot.

"Should we make flyers, maybe?" Harper asks. She holds

her hands in front of her face, miming a headline. "Found cat. Very cute, incredibly fat. Reward for finding her: ten million dollars."

I let a small laugh escape. "We can't charge anyone for finding her. That counts as blackmail, I think."

"Yeah, you're right." Harper laughs and turns off the computer. "What do you want to do now?"

Oh no, here it is. I like hanging out with Harper, but we don't have anything left to do. And I still can't really talk, so she'll definitely think I'm weird and then—

"Wanna see the cat before we go home?" Harper asks.

My panic evaporates, and my muscles relax. Harper's not like Nic; we can always talk about Phantom. I owe a lot to that little cat. "Yeah. Let's go."

Chapter 14

I take a deep breath before stepping into the lunchroom. I have to get Phantom's turkey sandwich, but today's a bad day. It happens sometimes—I get anxious for no reason, and my body is sweaty and twitchy. It's probably because I have to go to Nic's house tomorrow and dress up. It's almost like a date! Except Dad will be there. And Nic doesn't like me like that. I think.

I rub the hem of my shirt between my fingers. I don't know what's going on with Nic at all. Why is she being so nice to me? Does she want to be friends? But why? I don't get it. I don't get why she'd try so hard to be friends with someone as weird as me.

I get Phantom's sandwich and a fruit cup for me, and

I'm headed to the theater when Nic waves at me from her table. She's sitting with Emily and Amberleigh, as always. Amberleigh is the most popular kid in school. Nic is number two.

"Avery! Come here, come here."

I hesitate, my knuckles pale against the fruit cup. Nic seems happy to see me, but Emily seems indifferent and Amberleigh looks like she stepped in something disgusting. But Nic's smile makes my feet move, and soon I'm standing in front of her table.

I open my mouth to ask her what's up, but Amberleigh's and Emily's stares freeze the words in my throat.

"Come sit with us," Nic says, rescuing me. She flashes a brilliant smile. "You always sit by yourself outside. And we can discuss our plans for tomorrow!"

"What plans?" Amberleigh asks, one eyebrow raised. Any liquid I have left in my mouth dries up in a second.

Nic is completely oblivious. "Avery's gonna practice for the play at my house. She's Juliet, remember?"

"Oh yeah." Amberleigh looks me up and down, the one

eyebrow still raised. How does she keep it like that for so long? "Congrats."

"So, come on." Nic pats the stool next to her.

My brain is short-circuiting. This is too much. I can't take sitting at the table with the girl I like, and her popular friend, and one of the people who thinks I'm a terrible Juliet, *and* I only have a fruit cup that I can't eat because I can't eat when I'm anxious and anxiety is eating the lining of my stomach like the old-school *Pac-Man* game eats those white marbles—

"Avery?" Nic's smile fades a little.

"I can't," I squeak. "I have to—I have to—" My breath is already short. I wave weakly and then hurry away from her table.

Not fast enough.

"Who was that?" Amberleigh's voice reaches me. "She's so weird."

I sprint out of the cafeteria so Nic won't see the tears building in my eyes.

I go straight to Phantom's closet. I open the door, but

she's not in her bed. I get to my knees, trying not to cry. "Phantom? You there?"

I hear a meow, and Phantom emerges from the hole. She climbs into my lap, bumping her cold head against my chin.

"Where do you go anyway?" I hug her, and she licks my cheek. She meows in my ear and looks at her food bowl. Point taken.

I put her down and open the turkey sandwich bag. Phantom's ears prick, and she goes to her food bowl, already licking her lips. I take the turkey off the bread and place it in her bowl. She wolfs it down and looks at me for more.

"Sorry, that's all I got." I watch her clean her whiskers, feeling low. "I'm having a hard time, Phantom. That's what Dad used to say when we lived at the apartment."

"What happened?"

I look back in response to Harper's voice. I didn't hear her coming, again. She's as quiet as Phantom. She has her hands in her pockets and is leaning against the back of the stage. Phantom prances over to Harper with her tail straight up the air and starts circling her ankles.

"Hey, cat," she says, petting Phantom. She looks up and gives me a nervous smile. "I saw you running from the lunchroom. But if you don't want to talk, that's okay. You can tell me to get lost."

I wait for the panic to overwhelm me like usual, but there's nothing. I'm still feeling rotten, even though Phantom helped. Maybe I do need to talk.

"It's okay." I sit down next to the closet, and Harper sits next to me. Phantom climbs into my lap, yawning.

Harper crosses her legs. "I saw you talking to the popular gang. They're mean, so don't worry about what they said."

"Nic's not mean." I wince when I hear the defensiveness in my voice. "She's really cool. It's not her fault, it's mine."

"Your fault that you're upset?" Harper's tone is skeptical.

"Well, no. Amberleigh called me weird." I rub Phantom's soft ears. "And I guess I am."

"Why? Because you can't talk to people easy?" When I nod, Harper shrugs. "You're talking fine now."

Huh. I suppose so. I look at Harper, and she gives me a little smile. Maybe Nic was right. Phantom's in my lap, asleep, and now I'm calmer. I don't feel even a little sweaty. Maybe her Noodle plan will work.

Harper's stomach growls. She wraps one arm around her middle and sighs. "Well, that's embarrassing."

"Do you want my fruit cup?" I hold it out to her. "I'm not hungry."

Harper stares at it for a second, an expression I've never seen before crossing her face. Fear? Hunger? Something in between? "Are you sure?"

"Yeah, go ahead. When I get anxious, I can't eat."

Harper takes the fruit cup, opens it, and swallows the whole thing in a few seconds. I watch her in awe. I don't think she even chewed it.

"Thanks," she says, licking her lips. She hesitates, dragging her thumbnail over the plastic edge. "I didn't bring anything for lunch today."

Or the last time I saw her. I frown down at my hands. Before Dad got his new job, some months we were short and he wouldn't eat lunch. Maybe January is a short month for Harper's family too.

"I hardly ever eat my lunch," I say, "so you can have some of mine if you want." Harper looks a little irritated so I quickly say, "It's not charity. I literally throw it away every day."

"If you don't eat, you're gonna blow away!" Harper says, smiling. "But thanks, Avery. You're okay."

Warmth fills my empty stomach. In Harper's eyes, I'm okay. That's, like, maybe four steps away from real friendship. The closest I've been in over a year!

The lunch bell rings, and Harper slaps her forehead. "Shoot, we should have talked about Phantom! Can you meet me tomorrow?"

My stomach does a somersault when I think of my Friday plans. "Uh, no. But maybe Saturday?"

"Deal. Give me your phone." I do, and Harper hastily types in her number. She gives it back to me, smiling. "Text me, and we'll find Phantom's owner! Promise."

I hold my phone like it's a diamond. Hanging out with Nic tomorrow, then Harper on Saturday. It's too good to be true.

It's almost like I'm normal.

Chapter 15

Dad and I stand outside Nic's house. I'm nervous, my dress's armpits already damp. But even Dad seems nervous. He keeps messing with his tie and the buttons on his shirtsleeve.

"You okay?" I ask him.

Dad smiles down at me. "I'm okay. Ready?"

I nod and Dad rings Nic's doorbell.

Immediately, a thunderous barking starts, followed by "Noodle! Hush, be quiet!"

A tall woman opens the door. She's wearing a pretty red dress and red lipstick and golden hoop earrings. She's gotta be the prettiest woman I've ever seen. A man comes up behind her, wearing a dress shirt but also gray sweatpants.

He smiles at Dad warmly. Nic waves at me from behind them, holding on to Noodle's collar. I wave back shyly.

"You must be Mr. Williams," Nic's mom says with a smile. "I'm Carol, Nic's mom. And this is my husband, Kevin." They all shake hands, saying "Hi" and "Hello" and "Nice to meet you." Dad looks even more nervous than before. I know the feeling, Dad.

"Nice to meet you," Dad says, his voice a little squeaky. "I'm Charles. Umm, Avery's dad."

"Guys," Nic hisses, nudging her mom's side. She's still holding Noodle, who's straining to get to me and Dad, tail wagging. "Let them in already!"

Nic's dad laughs and moves to the side. I hesitate, but Dad puts a hand behind my head and nudges me forward. "Be strong," he murmurs. But it's almost like he's talking to himself.

Nic's house is like her family—big and warm. The walls in the living room are covered in pictures. An old woman (maybe Nic's grandma?) sits on her couch, fast asleep, while a toddler plays with red and yellow blocks at her feet.

Nic lets Noodle go as soon as the door swings shut behind us. The dog runs to me, whining and licking my arms and legs and chin. I laugh, some of the anxiety in my stomach dissolving, and pet her behind her floppy ears.

"Avery," Dad groans, "don't let the dog lick you in the face. At least."

Before I can answer, Nic's mom glares pointedly at her. "I thought we were going to keep the dog in your room, Nic."

"We are!" Nic says, grinning. "Avery and I will go upstairs and you guys can talk. Okay?"

Dad and I look at each other at the same time. His eyebrows scrunch together. "You'll be okay?"

"I'll be okay."

"Good!" Nic says, grabbing my hand. I try my best not to melt into a useless puddle. "Come on, let's go upstairs."

Nic leads me through the kitchen, Noodle trotting behind us. It's messy, dishes piled in the sink, loose papers all over the counter and a small island in the middle. It's different from our kitchen; ours is still spotless from the move. Dad hasn't even had time to put his magnet collection up.

"Sorry it's so messy," Nic says as we head toward shiny hardwood stairs. "I forgot to tell Mom you and your dad were coming over, so now she's kinda mad at me."

So what was that text? Did she not ask her mom right then? Heat builds in my face. Did Nic want me to come over that bad?

Nic has her foot on the first step when a kid appears at the top. He comes down, and I realize I've seen him before. He's in eighth grade, and I think he's on the football team. I didn't know he was Nic's brother.

"Oh, who's this?" he says when he's halfway down the stairs. I feel my throat closing up, but I put a hand on Noodle's back and try to give him a smile. It's probably closer to a grimace though.

"Mind your own business, Jamal," Nic says, climbing the stairs. Jamal hops in front of her playfully, mimicking her movements as she tries to go around. "Ugh! Why are you like this?"

"Just trying to see my sister's first friend!"

First friend? I frown at Nic as she balls up her fists and

punches Jamal while he laughs. She's never had anyone come over before? But what about Amberleigh and Emily?

Nic finally scrambles away from Jamal. He shakes his head, still laughing, and passes me. He inclines his chin, smiling. "Watch out for Nicki. She's a lot."

"Come on, Avery," Nic calls me from the top of the stairs. "Just ignore him."

I manage to wave at Jamal as he goes into the kitchen, and hurry upstairs after Nic. There's a long hallway at the top, lined with rooms. Nic leads me to the second one on the right, a white door with a big heart decal in the middle. Below that is a handwritten sign that says ERIC, I WILL KILL YOU IF YOU GO IN MY ROOM.

Nic opens her door, and I'm momentarily stunned. I was expecting a lot of pink and white, but Nic's room is dark blue, the ceiling covered in stick-on stars. She has a big bed at the back, and a TV stand full of movies and games. She even has a skateboard propped up in one corner. Nic is way cooler than I thought.

"Sorry about Jamal," Nic says, sitting on the floor at the

foot of her bed. Noodle speeds to her side and tries to lick her face. She holds Noodle at arm's length, giggling.

I sit next to her. I try to find something to say. *Your room is so cool.* But maybe she would get offended because I expected something else? *You're so cool.* No, definitely not that. I wipe my hands on my pants. I'm all sweaty again.

Noodle leaves Nic and sits beside me, panting in my face. I pet Noodle, and little by little, I feel calmer. I take a deep breath. I've already talked to her once. Twice, actually, if we count before my panic attack. So, I can do it again.

"I have a brother too."

Nic raises her eyebrows. "Oh, so you know the pain?"

I smile a little. "Yeah. Andrew's a jerk."

"So is Jamal!" Nic sighs heavily. "Well, he's not so bad. I can't stand my little brother Eric. He's eight and he's the worst. He's always coming into my room and grabbing my stuff. If I don't keep an eye on my phone, he's got it. I just wanna . . ." Nic boxes the air in front of her.

I'm laughing now and not feeling so sweaty anymore. "How many brothers do you have?"

"Three. Jamal's thirteen, Eric's eight, and Q is just two. I'm the only girl. Boys everywhere. Isn't that awful?"

"Noodle's a girl," I offer, and Nic laughs.

"Yeah, true! She's better than all my brothers combined." Nic pauses for a moment, staring at me intently. The sweat starts up again.

"What?"

"I was right. It's working." Nic nods to herself, a satisfied expression on her face.

"What's working?"

"My idea with Noodle. You're talking to me great right now!"

I don't know what to say, so I pet Noodle's head. She's lying beside me now, her head in my lap. I do kinda feel calmer with Noodle here. But maybe I'm just getting used to Nic. We've talked a few times already and she's not so scary. She's still way too cool for me, but she's at least nice about it.

"I googled it," Nic says after my silence, "and it looks like you can get an emotional support animal to help with your anxiety. Have you ever heard of that?"

"I can't. My brother's allergic to cats and dogs."

"Ugh, right. Brothers ruin everything." Nic crosses her arms and frowns at the floor. "Maybe we can keep your pet here and you can pick it up on the way to school?"

I remember Nic's mom's glare at Noodle. "I don't think that'll work."

"Yeah, you're probably right. Mom's already mad at me, so I don't want to push it." Nic looks back at me and leans against her bed. "This is tough. But don't worry, Avery. We'll figure something out."

Warmth spreads from my head to my fingertips. "Thanks."

Nic looks away from me, almost shyly. "I'm really glad you trust me enough to talk to me."

Oh God. My heart hammers against my ribs and I feel short of breath, but this has nothing to do with anxiety. Is she trying to kill me?

"Girls, are you up here?" Nic's mom opens her door, and I pray she can't tell I'm about to have a heart attack. "Avery and her dad have to get going."

"Okay!" Nic jumps to her feet, and I stand too. She looks like she wants to give me a hug but stops herself. She grins at me instead. "Next time we'll practice for the play, okay?"

"Okay." I return her smile, pat Noodle's head one more time, and follow Nic's mom downstairs. Dad's waiting for me at the door. I think the meeting went well because he doesn't seem so stressed anymore.

"Ready?" he asks, and I nod. We wave goodbye to Nic's mom and dad and go to the car. We're halfway home before I muster the courage to speak.

"How'd it go?"

"Excellent. I think you'll be fine to hang out there." Dad loosens his tie a little, sighing. "But man, what a high-energy family."

I turn toward the window so he won't see me smile. "Yeah. But I think I like that."

Chapter 16

I leave for school on Monday, and Nic's waiting by my house.

At first, I think I'm dreaming. But even after I blink a few times and pinch myself, she's still there. She waves, and I wave back tentatively.

"Move out the way," Andrew grunts behind me. Before I can move, he pushes past me. He stops for a second when he sees Nic, then smirks at me. "Aww, your friend is here to walk you to school. How sweet."

"Shut up," I growl, my face burning. I hurry to Nic's side before he has a chance to say anything else.

"Hey!" she says when I get closer. "I hope it's okay if we walk to school together. You do walk sometimes, right?"

"Yeah," I say, but my tone is all wrong. I'm still irritated by Andrew. What's it to him if Nic comes to walk to school together?

Nic glances behind me. "Is that your brother?"

"Yeah."

"He definitely looks like a jerk."

I smile, some of the irritation melting away. "He is. Why aren't you riding the bus?"

"I thought we could practice for the play while we walk!" Nic pulls out her script. It's banged up and crumpled, and the back has a mysterious brown stain at the bottom. "We should get in as much practice as possible. Class practice isn't good for you, at least not yet, and I don't think your dad would let you come to my house *every* day, so this is perfect."

She's really dedicated to this play. I feel a stab of regret— I haven't thought about the play at all this weekend. I *have* been thinking about how much I wanted to see Nic again though, so I guess it works out.

"Okay. Let's do it." I pull out my script, which is still

pretty much brand-new except for my sweaty handprints. "Umm, where should we start?"

"Let's start at act three." Nic flips to the back of the script. "We'll practice act one to death in class, and then acts two and three will suck. Happens every time."

I flip to the back slowly, guilt eating at me. Nic loves theater. Anyone can tell. And here I am with the lead part, and I'm just goofing off. I didn't do anything this weekend. I texted Harper about hanging out on Saturday, like she said, but she apologized and said something came up. I hope it's not that she changed her mind . . . After that, I just looked for pictures of lost-pet pictures online (no Phantom so far) and daydreamed about Nic telling me she liked me. No practice at all.

"Okay, I'll start," Nic says. She clears her throat, then looks intensely ahead of us. "Romeo is bad news."

"But I love him." Even I can hear that my voice is flat. Thomas's face pops into my head, and I shudder. I definitely do not love him, in any sense of the word.

"Love doesn't keep your mom from shutting down her

store," Nic says. There's a little bite to her words, as if she's really scolding me. "Don't you have any loyalty?"

"That has nothing to do with me!" I try to add some feeling, and I think it's working. I would be pretty upset if someone told me I couldn't like Nic because of donuts or whatever. Or, er, something else, like being in the play? I don't know, I've confused myself now. I think I'm mixing my metaphors.

"That was really good!" Nic says, out of character now. "You do great when it's just our parts."

Well. There's a reason for that.

"Maybe I can read for Romeo?" Nic suggests. "Then just picture me instead of Thomas's dumb face."

That's not gonna work, considering I have to kiss Thomas's dumb face at the end of this play, and if I imagined kissing Nic's much prettier face, I would have a heart attack and die.

"I want to really nail our parts first," I say to cover my embarrassment. "If that's okay?"

"Yeah!" Nic says. "Let's keep going."

We run through the rest of the scene, then backtrack to a scene in act 2. I look up from the script for a second, but do a double take. Just a few feet ahead of us is a familiar pair of red Converse—Harper.

"Wait, Nic," I say, interrupting her. She looks up curiously. "Hang on a second."

I don't wait for Nic to answer. I jog to Harper's side. She's wearing her headphones, so I have to wave my hands in front of her before she notices me. She jumps, then gives me a small smile. "Hey, Avery. What's up?"

I suddenly don't know what to say. I just saw her and wanted to talk to her, but I didn't think about her canceling our plans on Saturday. "Oh, uh, just wanted to say hi."

Harper smiles. "Hey, again. Oh, and sorry about canceling on Saturday. My mom was being a real . . . jerk. Anyway, sorry."

My anxiety fades. I bet Harper's mom is like Dad—no new friends without parental approval. "Oh, that's okay! I get it. My dad's strict sometimes too."

A flash of discomfort lashes across Harper's face, but it's gone as soon as it appears. "Maybe a different day."

"Yeah, definitely." I wonder why Harper looked uncomfortable. Maybe she doesn't want to talk about it. Time for a subject change. "I didn't know you walked to school."

Harper puts one of her hands in her pockets. She's not wearing gloves. "Every day of my life."

"Oh." How come I've never seen her? "We're walking today too." I look at Nic, and Harper follows my line of sight. Nic looks shocked, and I realize she's never seen me talking to Harper. "Do you want to walk with us?"

Harper hesitates but then shrugs. "Sure."

I motion for Nic to join us. She catches up to us, glancing between me and Harper. "Hey! You're Harper, right?"

"Yep." Harper seems a little uninterested. Unease swirls in my stomach. Maybe this was a bad idea.

Nic looks at me. Her expression is hard to read. Anxious? Annoyed? I don't know. She's smiling, but it doesn't reach her eyes. "Are you and Harper . . . friends?"

I glance at Harper, nerves eating at my gut. Are we friends? We've only talked a few times. But I would like to be her friend, I think. She's cool and real, and I don't feel too bad when I talk to her, and we did exchange phone numbers—

"Yep," Harper says. She gives me an encouraging half smile. "We're friends."

Can I hug Harper right now? Is that allowed?

"Oh, cool." Nic doesn't look like it's cool. She looks kinda mad. "Can you practice with Harper around?"

I fiddle with my script. There's a weird tension in the air, and I have no idea how it happened. Maybe Nic doesn't like Harper? Or the other way around?

"Umm, I can try." I hold up the script. "Me and Nic are practicing our lines. I'm not very good at acting."

"Yet!" Nic says, some of her frostiness disappearing.

"You gotta be halfway decent," Harper says. We start walking again, Nic to my left, Harper to my right. "You're Juliet, ain't you?"

"She's a really good singer," Nic says.

Harper nods. "That makes sense. Though I never wanted it to be a musical."

"Really?" I ask. "Why'd you change it?"

"Mrs. Thompson made me. She wrote all the songs. Something about musicals selling better."

So I have Mrs. Thompson to thank for this mess, huh? If it hadn't been a musical, Nic would have been Juliet and I would have been in the crew like always. Curse her for doing this to me.

"No wonder the songs are so goofy. But I like the play," Nic says to Harper. "The characters are really good." Her tone is a little guarded, like she's unsure how Harper will take the compliment.

Harper shrugs. "They're okay. Honestly, as long as y'all have fun performing the play, I don't care how it turns out."

Harper is a strange girl, but I like her. There's an honesty in her words. She's kinda easygoing, but tense at the same time. Way different than Nic.

"Let's hear those lines," Harper says after a few seconds. "How bad of an actress are you?"

Normally I'd be embarrassed, but the words don't hurt from Harper. Nic and I go back and forth until we see the school in the distance.

"Not bad," Harper says. "I mean, not great, but you just need more practice. Think about how it feels to really be Juliet, you know? Like what does she like and how does that affect how she talks? That helps me when I write anyway."

Hmm. "Maybe you can tell me more about Juliet later? So I can get into character?"

Harper smiles. For the first time, I notice she's missing a tooth, way in the back. "You got it, friend."

When we reach the school, Harper waves at us and heads toward the science wing. Maybe I'll see her at lunch.

Nic watches her leave, that weird expression I can't identify back in full force.

"Umm . . ." I trail off, uncertain. Maybe I shouldn't ask. "See you in English?"

Nic looks back at me and her normal, happy expression returns. "Of course! We can practice more later too. Oh, and we gotta pick a day for you to come over!"

The first bell rings, so I don't get to answer. Nic has history first period, which is all the way across the school. She grimaces and takes off running, waving at me. I wave back, a funny feeling in my chest. I hope I didn't make a mistake introducing Nic and Harper. I hope I didn't ruin both friendships before they even started.

Chapter 17

Wanna come over tomorrow night to practice?

I stare at Nic's text. It's almost too good to be true. The prettiest girl in school, texting me. Wanting to help me practice. Walking with me to school! Maybe I didn't ruin everything. Who knew all I'd have to do to turn my luck around was suffer in the lead role of a play?

"What're you smiling at your phone for?" Andrew grunts from the couch. It's a rare night he's home. Dad's not back from work yet (even though it's seven already). I'm pretty sure Dad got onto him for not watching me, because he's been moping around a lot lately.

I try to channel Nic. "Mind your own business, Andrew."

He throws a pillow at me. Not exactly how Jamal responded.

I throw it back, but it whizzes past his head. He gives me an arrogant smile. "That's why you're in theater and not softball, I guess."

I don't have to take this. "I'm going to my room."

"Wait," Andrew says. He sits up, his expression uncommonly serious. "I need to ask you something."

Oh God. I can't even imagine what Andrew would want from me. "What? I'm not covering for you for a party or something."

Andrew snorts. "Like I'd need you to. No, this is about you."

"Me?"

Andrew looks into my eyes. "Is that girl who meets you before school your girlfriend?"

All the breath leaves my body at once. I'm hot and cold, and my legs itch to run away. No one knows that I like girls, except for my uncle Denny. And I only told him because he was drunk. Dad would kill me. Well, maybe not, but I don't know what he'd say. I can't tell him, at least not now. How did Andrew, of all people, guess?!

"I'm going to m-my room." I try to walk away, but my legs won't work all of a sudden. I'm glued to the spot.

"I'm just asking," Andrew says, his palms up. "I don't care if you like girls or whatever. It's not exactly a secret."

Confusion clouds my mind. "What . . . ? How did you know?"

Andrew rolls his eyes. "You used to look at my girlfriend like she was a superhero."

Heat fills my face. "That was a long time ago!"

"Two years ago."

I throw another pillow at him. This time I don't miss, and it nails him in the face. "Leave me alone! I can't believe this. You didn't tell Dad, did you?"

Andrew rubs his nose, his expression annoyed. "No, but you're being such a brat, I might."

Fear seizes my heart and tears jump in my eyes. "Please don't. Please."

Andrew's eyes soften. "It's okay, I won't. Dad wouldn't care though, you know."

I hesitate, staring at the floor. "I can't take that chance."

"Fair enough." Andrew picks up the pillows we tossed around and pats my head. His touch is heavy but warm. "Now answer your girlfriend's text. It's not cool to keep her waiting."

"Nic's not my girlfriend," I say, but he's already halfway upstairs. I pick up the phone and look at her text again. I let myself imagine, just for a second, what it would be like if Andrew was right and Nic really liked me the way I like her. It's almost too painful to bear. But I want to be close to her, if she'll let me. Even if I can just be her friend, I'll take it. I take a deep breath and type my response.

I'll be there.

After theater, I go to Phantom's closet.

Harper asked me to meet her here, and I hope that means she found something about Phantom. Well, I say hope, but I really don't know. Phantom's so cute, playing with the toy mouse I finally got her. I'm aching to just keep her with me forever.

"Avery?" Harper calls.

"Back here!"

Harper appears, poking her head behind the curtain cautiously. I wave at her, and she comes to my side. "Coast is clear! Ready to begin Operation Find the Cat's Owner?"

"What exactly are we doing?"

"So I was thinking—Phantom is here at lunchtime and just after school, right? Maybe that's because she knows you're here at those times. But she probably leaves after that."

"Okay . . . where does she go?"

"Let's find out. If we pretend to leave, we can spy on her and see where she goes." Harper leans down and pets Phantom. "We're leaving! See you later."

"Bye, Phantom." I pet her too. She purrs and rubs her face against my legs. I don't want to leave, but I pack up and put my backpack on. Phantom trots into her closet and flops onto her bed. I close the door, and Harper and I walk slowly off the stage. But as soon as we're out of the theater, we race to the back of it.

"There's the hole," I whisper, crouching behind a bush. It's hidden behind the air conditioner, so I guess no one noticed it. "How long do you think it'll take her to come out?"

"I have no idea. We just have to wait."

Harper and I stare at the hole intently for a few minutes, but Phantom doesn't come out. "Do you think she's taking a nap?"

"Maybe," Harper says, doubt in her voice. "I'm sorry. I thought this would work."

"It's okay. Cats have minds of their own."

"Yeah." Harper laughs a little, but it's nervous. "I don't really know that much about cats."

"Same here! I just think they're cute. We can't have pets because of my brother."

"I can't have pets either," Harper says. "But it's because it's not, er, practical."

Not practical? What does that mean? I don't get a chance

to ask though, because I see a pair of fuzzy gray ears poke out of the school.

"There she is!" Harper and I jump to our feet as Phantom emerges from the hole. She stretches, then trots away, the opposite direction of my house. Harper nods, her face determined. "Let's follow her."

Phantom leads us down three streets. She stops at an old apartment building to sniff at the dumpster but keeps moving after a few minutes. She also stops to hiss at a weenie dog barking behind a chain-link fence. She sits right next to the fence and starts cleaning her whiskers.

"Your cat's kinda mean," Harper says, laughing as the dog barks ferociously and claws at the fence.

"She's just teasing," I say, but I'm laughing too. Harper and I wait for several minutes in silence, but Phantom is lounging now, eyes closed while the dog tries to tear the fence down. "Hey, what'd you mean about pets not being practical?"

Harper fidgets a little. She doesn't look at me. "It's kinda complicated."

"Oh, sorry," I say quickly. Did I say something wrong? Am I ruining it? "I won't ask again."

"It's okay," Harper says. "It's just that my mom . . ." She trails off, looking behind me. "I think she's getting ready to move."

I turn around in time to see a woman come out of the house and yell at the barking dog. Phantom gets up and trots away. We follow her for a few more minutes until she reaches a pretty blue house with a big FOR SALE sign in the front yard. Phantom slips between a gap in the front steps and disappears. We wait, but she doesn't come out again.

"Do you think she lives here?" Harper asks me.

"Lived, maybe?" I point at the sign. "Looks empty."

"Hey, do you kids know the Romans?"

I turn in alarm as an old lady from next door peeks over her fence at us. I struggle for words, but Harper rescues me.

"No, ma'am. We were wondering if anyone still lived here."

The old lady shakes her head. "Moved out two months ago. Not very nice people. I hope someone nicer moves in. Are you interested?"

I shake my head, and Harper laughs. "No, we're just passing by. Actually, we were looking for a cat. Have you seen it? It's gray and kinda fat."

The lady nods. "Yes, I've seen that thing around. Can't stand it, chases all my birds away! But I do feel a little sorry for it. The Romans left the poor thing behind when they moved."

Well, that answers that. We thank the old lady and leave, headed back to school.

"What do we do now?" I ask Harper when we're safely away from the old lady. "Phantom doesn't have an owner. I can't believe they'd leave her." I hate to leave Phantom in that big empty house, but I guess she's been fine for two months.

"I know! People are horrible." Harper crosses her arms and looks up at the sky. "I guess she's your cat now, right? You're already taking care of her."

Joy overwhelms me. She really is my cat now. "Yeah. I guess she is."

"But we shouldn't tell anyone," Harper says as the school comes into view. "Even Nic."

Why not? I mean, I get why we wouldn't tell Mrs. Thompson or an adult, but why Nic specifically? Harper seemed kinda uneasy around Nic . . . But I don't want to ask her about it. It can be our secret for now. "Okay. Deal."

Harper and I say goodbye. I check my phone, and my stomach drops. It's already four thirty! And I'm supposed to go to Nic's! I shoulder my backpack and wave to Harper. "See you tomorrow!"

She smiles. "See ya."

Chapter 18

I hesitate outside Nic's door. I ran all the way here in a panic, but now I'm nervous. I already texted Dad and told him I'd be at Nic's though, so I can't chicken out. Still, I'm sweaty again, and Andrew calling Nic my girlfriend won't leave my head.

Okay, Avery. Be cool. You can do this. I try to breathe deeply, but my lungs aren't cooperating. I settle for a half breath and ring Nic's doorbell.

Noodle immediately starts barking. There's some cursing, and then Nic's mom answers the door, holding Noodle's collar. She's visibly shocked to see me. "Oh, Avery! What're you—

"Is that Avery?" Nic thunders down the stairs and appears

behind her mom. She grins at me. "Hey! Sorry, Mom, forgot to tell you Avery was coming over. Come in!"

Nic's mom moves to the side so I can get in. She looks exasperated. "Nic, I told you to let me know when you have friends over. The house is a wreck—"

"We'll be in my room!" Nic tugs at my hand and pulls me inside.

I nod weakly to Nic's mom and let Nic rush me upstairs. Noodle follows at our heels, panting.

"Where were you?" Nic asks when we're safely in her room. She closes her door, muffling the sound of heavy bass coming from the next room. "It's five o'clock!"

"I hang out after school sometimes," I say. I almost tell her about Phantom, but I hold it in. Harper asked me not to tell, and I won't. Though I'm dying to tell Nic. She'd love something like this.

Nic accepts my explanation with a nod. "Okay, let's get to work! Did you bring your script?"

We run through our lines in act 2 and 3. I'm comfortable

with them now, I think. They're familiar at least. Maybe I could read out loud in class finally?

"That was really good!" Nic says as we finish reading. "Now, I know we've been just saying the song lyrics, but maybe we should sing them."

I shake my head, panic clawing up my throat. "I . . . I can't."

"Not even with Noodle?"

I look at Noodle, who's been chewing on a plastic bone. She looks at me, licking her whiskers. "I don't think so."

"Hmm." Nic taps her finger on the back of her script. "How'd you sing in front of Mrs. Thompson?"

"She let me close my eyes."

"That's not gonna work. You can't do the whole play with your eyes closed."

My lungs are getting that can't-breathe feeling. She's right, I can't do this with my eyes closed. I can't sing in front of an audience. I'll pass out. I'll die. Dad will be so disappointed.

"Avery?" Nic leans closer, her expression anxious. "You okay? You don't look so good."

"I'm okay," I gasp. My lungs are closing up. I close my eyes and focus on breathing and the exercise Nurse Biles makes me do. I can't do sight right now. Three things I can touch it is.

"Noodle," I mutter, running my hands through her fur. "My jeans. Carpet."

The panic subsides enough so I can breathe again. Tentatively, I open my eyes again. Nic's close, almost too close, watching my face anxiously.

"Was that a panic attack?" she asks, her voice hushed.

"Almost." I give her a wobbly smile. "Caught it in time."

Nic seems relieved. She sits back down, her arms crossed. "Well, no singing for now. Let's get something to eat, and we can try again later."

My stomach drops at the thought of trying to sing again, but I nod anyway. My legs are a little shaky when I stand, but hopefully Nic doesn't notice.

We go downstairs, and Nic marches to the kitchen. A little kid's doing his homework at the counter, but his eyes light up when he sees Nic.

"Can I play on your phone?" he asks.

"Get lost," Nic growls. She turns to me, rolling her eyes. "This is Eric, my monster of a little brother. Better watch your phone. He'll grab it."

"Hi," he says to me, his voice dripping with sweetness. "What's your name? You shouldn't be Nic's friend. She's mean—"

"Dad," Nic bellows. "Can you get Eric out of here? Please?"

"He was there first," Nic's dad calls from somewhere in the living room. Eric sticks his tongue out at Nic.

Nic looks like she'll explode at any minute. I can't help but laugh. I've never seen Nic frustrated before. She's cool and kind at school, but it's nice to see this side too.

"Fine. You can play for *ten* minutes if you'll leave. Then I'm coming to get it." Nic gives Eric her phone, and he runs upstairs, abandoning his homework. She turns to me, shaking her head. "I have got to get out of this madhouse. Do you like popcorn?"

"Yeah." I sit at the counter, next to Eric's homework. "Can I have some water too?"

"Sure!" Nic pops some popcorn for us in the microwave and brings me a glass of water. She sits next to me, shoving Eric's homework out of the way. She takes a few pieces of popcorn and sighs. "Do you ever think of running away from home?"

I smile and take a piece. It's sweet—kettle corn. "I used to. But Andrew's been kinda cool lately. It's weird."

"If only!" Nic sighs again, extra dramatic.

I watch her out of the corner of my eye. Nic's staring into her water glass, her eyes far away. She's pretty up close, but she has a tiny scar near her ear, and the beginnings of a pimple by her nose. I don't know why, but it makes me like her a little more. Andrew's words reverberate through my head, and I look back at my own water glass.

"Do you think practicing in the morning before school helps?" Nic asks after we've eaten almost all the popcorn.

I'm reminded of Harper. I wonder what Nic's feelings are. And Harper was adamant about us not telling her about Phantom. Is there something going on between them I don't know about? She's in a better mood, her eyes bright and happy. Maybe I can ask now. "Yeah, but . . . can I ask you something?"

"Anything." Nic leans closer, like we're about to share a secret.

"What do you think about Harper?"

Nic's eyes widen a little. She leans back, a frown replacing her smile. Uh oh. Maybe I shouldn't have asked.

"Sorry," I say quickly, "I was just curious since she's been walking with us and helping me out."

"No, it's okay!" Nic says. She picks at the edge of the counter, not looking at me. "I think she's pretty cool."

She doesn't *sound* like she thinks that. "But?"

"There's no but." Nic hesitates, and then continues. "Okay, maybe a little but. I was just surprised that you were friends with her."

"Why?"

"Well, I mean, you have such a hard time talking . . ."

"Oh." I feel a stab of pain. Does Nic think I'm that pathetic? Well, I guess I am, but still. I guess I was hoping she wouldn't notice I was hopeless at making friends.

"Sorry, I didn't mean to hurt your feelings." Nic looks anxious now. "I'm glad you're friends with her! And I really do think she's cool. She's got this intense artist vibe."

That pulls a smile out of me. "Yeah, that's true. I can't believe she wrote that play all by herself."

"Right?" Nic looks wistfully at the refrigerator. "I wish I had a talent like that."

What's she talking about? She's a really great actress. Even when we're running through our lines, she's acting things out and her inflection is perfect. She doesn't have to struggle to get into character. And she can sing really great too. Who cares if she's an alto? Mrs. Thompson, I guess, but that's not fair. I open my mouth to tell her all this, but Nic's mom pops her head into the kitchen.

"Avery, your dad is here to pick you up."

Dang it, Dad. I look at Nic, and she gives me a thumbs-up. "We'll practice the songs next time, okay?"

"Okay." I get my backpack from her room and meet Dad at the door. He rumples my hair when he sees me.

"Did you have fun?"

I look back at Nic, who waves. I wave back, my chest not as light as normal. Does Nic secretly think I'm weird because I don't have many friends? Does she think I'm hopeless? Does she just feel sorry for me, and that's why she was shocked about Harper? I look back at Dad, trying to put it out of my mind.

"Yeah. I did."

Chapter 19

I buy two sandwiches today.

One is for Phantom, as usual. But I think Harper would like to have more than a fruit cup. I'm not that hungry, so she can have the sandwich, if she wants it. I hope she likes turkey.

It's been a few days since I went to Nic's house. The weird way Harper and Nic acted the morning they met, and the conversation I had with Nic about it, has been nagging at me all week. Nic said she was surprised I had friends (which is still ouch), but Harper acted strange too. I'm gonna ask Harper about it. She'll be honest with me, I'm sure. But the problem is, do I want to know the answer?

I run from the lunchroom as quick as I can, before Amberleigh and Emily notice me. And Nic too. The "weird" comment still stings, and I don't want to think about how Nic feels about me. I go to the back of the theater, and Phantom meets me, meowing and purring.

"Okay, okay, turkey time. I know." I take off the bread and feed her the lunch meat. Her sharp teeth graze my fingertips as she gobbles it down. "Hey, chill! You're gonna take my fingers off."

Phantom responds by climbing into my lap and purring. I scratch behind her ears, and she closes her eyes. Her fur's dirtier than usual. She needs a bath, bad.

"Do you think Nic really wants to be my friend?" Phantom blinks sleepily at me. "Oh, you haven't met Nic. She's really cool. Way cooler than me. But she said she was surprised Harper was my friend. Hurt my feelings, even if it was true."

Phantom yawns. I guess she's not interested in my problems. "Well, what about you? What were your old owners like?" I ask her. "Were they mean to you? I hope not. But you're safe now, don't worry."

Phantom presses her paws against my legs, still purring. I wait for the pinpricks from her claws, but I don't feel them. I hold up one of her front paws and push the soft pad underneath. No claws pop out.

"Ugh, they declawed you *and* left you alone?! If I see them, I'll fight them."

"Who're you fighting?" Harper appears from behind the curtain. I never hear her coming. She'd be a great spy.

"Phantom's owners. Look." I pick Phantom up and show Harper Phantom's paws. "They declawed her!"

Harper sits next to me. She doesn't have a lunch again. "Is that bad?"

"Yeah! She can't catch food by herself anymore. She'll starve if we don't feed her."

Harper pokes Phantom's big belly. Phantom opens her eyes and nuzzles her face against Harper's hand. "I think we have some time before that happens."

I can't help but laugh. I don't know why anyone would leave her, especially if they liked her enough to feed her so much. But, even though it's kind of terrible, I'm secretly glad the Romans did, so I could find her.

"Oh, Harper, speaking of food . . ." I pull out Harper's sandwich and fruit cup, and give it to her. "Do you like turkey?"

Harper's eyes widen. "You don't have to give me that."

"I know, but I'm not that hungry."

"Well, you gotta eat something." Harper crosses her arms. "I won't take all your food."

Hmm. "I have this." I show her Phantom's leftover sandwich, which is soggy white bread and no turkey.

Harper doesn't look too happy but accepts the turkey sandwich and fruit cup anyway. "You're really just eating bread?"

"I like bread," I lie, taking a bite out of the leftovers. Somehow the lingering turkey taste makes it worse.

"Man," Harper says, laughing as she opens the fruit cup. "You are weird."

I freeze in the middle of biting my two pieces of bread. Not Harper too. No, I'm sure she's kidding. She laughed. I force myself to swallow the dry bread, but I'm not hungry. "Hey, Harper, do you really think I'm weird?"

"For eating two pieces of bread as a sandwich? Yeah."

"No, I mean . . ." I struggle to put my thoughts into words. "I mean, like, in general."

Harper finishes the fruit cup and starts on the sandwich. "Someone's been making fun of you, huh?" When I don't answer, she continues. "You're not weird. You just have anxiety. So what? Can't change it, can you?"

"Dad said I'd outgrow it."

Harper snorts. She's already done with the sandwich. "Outgrowing it eventually isn't doing you a lot of good right now though, is it?"

I lean back on my hands. I guess she's right. I can't change it, so if people think I'm weird, there's nothing I can do about that either. Maybe it's okay if Nic and Harper think I'm weird, as long as it's in a good way. But I don't want them to feel sorry for me.

"Who was it?" Harper asks. She's not smiling anymore. "Was it Nic?"

"Oh, no way! She'd never say that."

Harper grunts like she doesn't believe me. "She hangs out with Amberleigh and them, so you never know. I guess she's okay though."

It clicks then—Harper thought Nic was making fun of me. That's why she was acting so strange that morning. "Nic is a good friend, don't worry. I mean, I think we're friends. I never asked, technically, but we hang out sometimes and we practice for the play and she's pretty nice to me—"

"Stop," Harper says, smiling at me. "You and Nic are friends. You and me are friends. Don't overthink it."

I've never wanted to hug someone so much in my life. "Thanks, Harper."

The bell rings signaling the end of lunch. We get to our feet, and Phantom goes back into the closet, yawning. "No, Avery," she says, holding out her hand for a fist bump. I touch my fist to hers tentatively, and she gives me a half smile. "Thank you."

Chapter 20

I check my phone after theater, and I'm shocked by a notification from Dad.

Off from work early! I'm out front now.

Now? Like right now? Is something wrong? Pinpricks of sweat pop out against my hairline as I stuff my script into my backpack. I run out of the theater, my heart in my throat. Sure enough, his truck is parked in front of the building. He sees me and waves.

Some of the panic fades. He's grinning, so maybe nothing's wrong. I go to the truck and open the back door. "What're you doing here, Dad?"

"Geez, what a welcome." Dad laughs. "Come sit up front."

Uh oh. This isn't good. I'm about to get some bad news. I close the back door and climb into the passenger seat, dread in my stomach. What could it be? Did Dad get fired? Are we moving again? Dad doesn't look upset though. He's humming along with the radio and starts the car.

"Seat belt!" he says, his voice cheerful. I buckle up, uncertain. Maybe it's good news instead. "I know you're surprised, but nothing's wrong. Someone pulled the fire alarm at work, and they let us go early."

All the unease disappears in an instant. It is good news! "Did the sprinklers go off and everything?"

"Yep." Dad looks really happy as he pulls out of the school's parking lot. "My boss's computer is ruined."

"Serves him right for making you work so much."

Dad's smile fades a little. "Yeah. Sorry we haven't gotten to hang out as much."

"That's okay." And I really do mean it. I know he has to work. That's why I'm doing this play thing, so he won't worry about me while he's busy.

"How's the play going?" Dad asks. We should be almost

home, but he's driving down that abandoned road again. Why? "No more panic attacks?"

"No," I say, thinking about my almost one in Nic's room. "I know all my lines now. It's not so bad."

"Oh, good! I can't wait to see it."

I narrow my eyes at him. Something's weird. He's still smiling, but it's not reaching his eyes. He keeps glancing at me too. "Dad? What's wrong?"

"Nothing's wrong," he says quickly. Too quickly. "I just wanted to talk a bit."

"About what?"

"Well, I was talking to Nurse Biles earlier this week."

Why? I haven't seen her since the panic attack.

"I was also talking to your theater teacher, Mrs. Thompson. She says you're doing really well in class, but sometimes she worries about you." Dad takes a deep breath. "And I think, maybe, we should try something to help you with your anxiety."

Try something? Nervous heat creeps up my neck. "Like what?"

Dad doesn't look at me. "Like maybe talking to someone about it."

I gasp out loud. At first, I can't even think. What does "talking to someone" mean? Like therapy? Does anyone my age even go to therapy? I thought it was just for adults. Will people think I'm weird if I go? They already think I'm weird. Amberleigh said so.

"Avery?" Dad's voice is tentative.

And who is going to take me to therapy if I go? Dad already works so much and he's so tired all the time. Would he get in trouble with his boss? Would I have to miss school? If I missed school, everyone would find out. I'd be the weird girl who can't talk and has to miss first period because she can't control her anxiety like a normal person.

"Avery?" Dad's voice is more insistent now. "Are you okay?"

I can't breathe. I'm hot and sweaty, and the inside of Dad's truck is too cramped. But I can't have a panic attack now. That will just prove his point—that I can't take care of myself like everyone else can.

"I don't want to go." I force the words to sound strong,

even though my hands are shaking. I hide them in the sleeves of my jacket.

"Avery—"

"I'm fine. I don't need any therapy." Good thing he's driving so he can't see my face. I'm barely holding the attack back.

"It's just an idea," Dad says, glancing at me. "I'm just worried about you, Avery. It scares me when it gets bad."

I don't say anything because I'm trying to breathe. I remember Nurse Biles's exercises. Three things I can see. My backpack, Dad's blue coat, a million cows in a field. Three things I can feel. The warm leather of the seat, the breeze from the vents, my fingernails squeezed into my palms. Slowly, the heat fades and my throat opens up. I close my eyes, still shivering. See? I don't need therapy. I can do this by myself.

"Okay. I'll make you a deal," Dad says after a few minutes of silence. "We'll table the discussion for now. You said you're doing well in the play, and I believe you. But if it gets worse, we'll try again, okay?"

I take a deep, shaky breath. I have to stay in the play now. The stakes are too high. "Okay."

"Good deal." Dad pats my arm gently. "Let's go home and get pizza, yeah? Thin-crust pepperoni."

I nod, but I don't feel like eating. All I can think about is the fact that I can't sing in front of people yet. And I only have four weeks to fix that.

Chapter 21

After school the next day, I visit Phantom. She's sleeping in her bed, but when she sees me, she meows and practically climbs up my leg.

"Nice to see you too!" I pick her up and hold her at arm's length. "Phantom. Serious question. Do you think I need therapy?"

Phantom blinks at me. Is that a maybe?

"Nic said I needed a therapy animal. So maybe I'm just one step away from actual therapy. But I don't want to go."

Phantom reaches her paws out to me, meowing. I cradle her in my arms like a baby.

"I don't know, Phantom. It's confusing. I just want to

make this play work, you know? If I can just do that, everything will work out. I know it."

She extends one paw and touches my nose. My heart melts into a puddle of goo. I love this cat so much.

"You're right, let's forget about it. Let's take a picture." I hold Phantom up and take a selfie of us. Phantom's looking right at the camera, her eyes bright and adorable. I bury my face in her fur. I've got to find a way to take her home.

After a few moments, Phantom squirms out of my arms and hops to the ground. She bats a water bottle cap around, her tail twitching.

"I wish I was a cat. Turkey, bottle caps, a nice bed . . ." I trail off, remembering what Nic said about practicing in front of someone. Phantom is perfect. She can't even talk, and she's not really paying attention anyway. "Hang on, listen to this." I grab my script and turn to the first song. It's when Juliet and Romeo meet and decide to see each other again. I put my headphones on, press play on the music, open my mouth, and sing.

When I'm done, Phantom yawns. Unimpressed, I guess.

"I know, I gotta get the high notes right. I'm a little flat. Let me try again."

This time, I make sure I breathe deep, from the bottom of my belly. I close my eyes and really feel the music, the beat Mrs. Thompson recorded for us thumping in my ears. It's perfect this time.

I open my eyes, expecting Phantom to be looking at me, but she's gone. I almost call for her, but stop myself. This has happened too many times before. I turn, dread in my stomach, and sure enough, Harper's standing right behind me. Phantom circles her legs, purring.

"Oh my God." Harper's eyes are huge. "Nic wasn't kidding. You really can sing."

"You could have told me you were listening." My face is so hot I'm scared I'll disintegrate on the spot. But . . . I don't have that about-to-pass-out feeling. Maybe it's okay if Harper hears me sing?

Harper crosses the room and surprises me by grabbing my hands. "You gotta try out for *American Idol*. And win a million dollars."

I burst out laughing, and Harper grins. I say, "Thanks, but I can't sing in front of people. I get all sweaty."

"You can just wear extra deodorant!" Harper lets go of my hands, and Phantom returns to her bed. I close the closet door so she can nap, and Harper and I walk to the front of the theater. I'm cooling down now, and I'm not panicking. I guess I can add Harper and Phantom to the safe-to-sing-in-front-of list.

"What were you doing?" I ask.

"Coming to see if you'd gone home yet. Missed you yesterday." Harper hesitates, like she's about to tell me something but changes her mind. "Good thing too. I got to hear a concert."

"Stop!" We laugh some more. It's kind of nice, not having to worry about anything with Harper. We've been friends for a little over a week and I don't get too nervous around her.

"Do you want to walk home together?" I ask. Now that I think about it, I have no clue where Harper's house is. She has to live near me and Nic to meet us walking.

Harper's smile disappears. She looks down at her lap. "I'm not sure."

Did I say something wrong? "Not sure about . . . ?"

Harper meets my eyes. Hers are sad. "I'm not sure if I should go home."

I stay quiet for a second. Harper wears the same hoodie every day, and she doesn't bring lunch. And now she doesn't want to go home. I touch my phone. I can ask Dad if she can stay with me, but I'm sure he'll say yes. "Harper, do you want to—"

I'm interrupted by the door to the theater opening. We both look up—it's Nic. I start to wave, but my hand freezes halfway. She's wiping her eyes and sniffling. She's crying.

"Uh oh," Harper murmurs. "Better talk to her."

I want to, but I'm suddenly nervous. I've never seen Nic sad. What do I say? Harper nudges my arm, and I hop off the stage. I take a few steps closer, but it takes a while to work up the courage to speak.

"Nic? Are you okay?"

Nic looks up at us in alarm. She wipes her eyes with

the sleeve of her sweater. "Oh, hi, Avery. I—I thought the theater would be empty."

"We're always haunting the place." Harper jumps off the stage and joins my side. "What happened?"

Nic looks at the floor. "Nothing."

Harper and I exchange a look. Harper's eyebrow is raised.

"You don't have to talk about it." I hesitate but put a hand on Nic's arm. She looks up at me. Her eyes are red and watery still. My chest aches with sympathy and anger. What made Nic cry? Or who? It had to be something bad; Nic doesn't seem like a person who would let things get to her.

"Who did it?" Harper says. She puts her fists up in a mock boxing stance. "Me and Avery'll beat 'em up."

I put my fists up too. "They won't see us coming!"

Nic stares at us for a second, then bursts into laughter. I can't help laughing too. I've never been in a fight, and I probably never will.

"Thanks, guys." Nic wipes her eyes again. Her eyes are clear now. "I'm okay, I promise. What're you doing here?"

"Avery was practicing, and I overheard her." Harper elbows me playfully. "She can really sing. You weren't kidding."

"I told you!" Nic looks at me, excitement all over her face. "Did you sing in front of Harper?"

"No, I was singing to . . . myself. Harper just overheard me."

"Ah, well. We can practice tonight!"

That reminds me. I turn to Harper. "Do you want to stay over tonight?"

Both Harper and Nic look shocked, but I'm determined. Harper seemed scared to go home. Dad might freak out, but this is an emergency.

"Uh . . ." Harper looks unsure. "I guess I could? Maybe? If that's okay?"

"It's okay." I make sure I'm looking into Harper's eyes. "I promise."

"Wait," Nic says. "What about if we do it at my house? Avery, your dad gets home late, right?"

Oh, that might be better. Then Dad won't be panicking

about me bringing her over without asking. And that means Nic doesn't mind Harper, if she's okay spending a whole sleepover with her. But me spending the night at Nic's? My heart starts beating a bit faster at the thought.

"Is that okay?" Harper asks, glancing at me.

"Yeah!" Nic says. She bounces from foot to foot. "Oh, wow, this will be so much fun! A sleepover!"

Harper seems overwhelmed, so I give her a reassuring smile, even though my heart is thumping against my ribs at the thought of spending the night with the girl I like.

"It'll be fun, don't you think?"

Harper nods. "Okay. Let's do it."

Chapter 22

We walk to my house first, to get clothes and sleeping bags. Once Dad texts me back saying it's okay (with an added *PLEASE call me if you need to come home*), I open my front door cautiously—I don't know if Andrew's around. Luckily, the house is dark and silent.

"Okay, we're clear." I open the door wide for Harper and Nic. They both look around as I turn the lights on. There's still moving boxes in the living room . . . oops. "My room's upstairs, but I haven't finished unpacking yet, so it's kinda messy."

"That's okay," Nic says, still looking around the living room. "Your house is cool. It's . . ."

"Empty," Harper says, touching a moving box. "How come you haven't unpacked yet?"

I look at my living room. We've been here six months, but it still doesn't feel like home. I look at the blue walls and leather couch and all the boxes and miss that cramped apartment so bad it hurts.

"I don't know," I tell Harper, and I mean it. I try to shake the ache in my chest. "Anyway, let's go upstairs. Gotta get my sleeping bag."

We climb the steps to my room. It's messy, but thank goodness I don't have any underwear lying around.

"Your room is so cute!" Nic says, picking up a plush cat Dad got me for Christmas. Harper stands at the door but doesn't come in.

"Thanks." I hope to God she can't see the heat in my face. I grab a bunch of clothes, enough for me and Harper, and stuff them into my only duffel bag. My sleeping bag is somewhere . . . I look in my closet and under my bed, but it's not there. Probably packed up somewhere in one of the boxes.

"You like Pokémon?" Nic asks. She points at the poster of the original 151 above my bed. It used to be Andrew's, but he gave it to me after we moved.

"Yeah, Andrew and I used to play together, before he turned into a jerk." Wait, is Pokémon a weird thing to like?

"I like it too," Harper says. She's still standing at the door. "I didn't get to play the new games though."

"I love it too! But I mostly play the phone one. I haven't played the one for the Switch yet." Nic grins at me. "What's your favorite type? I like water types."

"Dark types," Harper says.

I beam at them both. I had no idea they liked Pokémon. Or really, anything. We haven't talked about a lot, I guess. "I like electric and grass types."

"Avery? Is that you?"

I groan. Andrew. "I'm upstairs. But I'm leaving soon."

Andrew comes up the stairs and pokes his head into my room. He raises his eyebrows when he sees Harper and Nic. "Oh, wow, first one friend, now another? Didn't know you had it in you."

"Go away!" I want to throw something at him, but I don't want to accidentally hit Harper. "I'm spending the night with Nic. Dad said I could. So you can leave."

"Oh, already?" Andrew wiggles his eyebrows at me, and I just want to kill him. "Okay, I see you!"

I pick up my pillow. "Harper, duck."

Andrew runs away as I hurl my pillow at him. I hear him laughing all the way to his room.

I turn to Nic and Harper, my face burning. "Ready to go?"

Harper nods, but Nic is staring at me with an expression I can't read. Did she guess what Andrew was talking about? Surely not, because he was vague, but what if she *did* guess? Oh, Andrew, I'm gonna kill you—

Nic smiles at me, and all the fear melts away. "Ready. Let's go, team! Sleepover time!" She grabs my hand, and I wish she'd hold on forever.

Chapter 23

"Okay, Avery, let's just try singing." Nic holds her beat-up script at eye level. "You can pick any song you want."

I nod, holding my script with shaking hands. Nic, Harper, and I are hanging out in Nic's room. We ate dinner already (pizza rolls, because Nic's mom was *not* happy about Nic not telling her about the sleepover in advance), and now it's play practice time. Specifically, singing time.

"Hang on to Noodle," Nic says. I put a hand on Noodle's head, but my whole body is trembling already.

Harper watches me in alarm. "Holy cow, is it always like this?"

"For now." Nic's voice has a defensive edge to it. "But she'll get better with practice, right?"

"Stop, stop." Harper surprises me by taking my script. I put my shaking hand back in my lap. "Avery, are you sure you can do this? You look like you're about to pass out."

"I have to do this." My voice is small. I think how many hours Nic has helped me practice, and my stomach clenches. I think about Dad and therapy, and I want to throw up.

"I think you should drop out. You look miserable."

Nic opens her mouth to protest, but I beat her to it. "I can't give up. I won't give up." There's too much to lose now.

Harper runs a hand through her hair. "All right. Well, maybe we need to start smaller. Can you sing in a group?"

"Like . . . karaoke?"

"Not what I meant, but that'll work. Give me your phone." I do and Harper taps on an app. She gives my phone back. It's on YouTube. "Pick a song, and me and Nic'll sing. You can join in if you want, but you don't have to."

I look to Nic, but she shrugs. Worth a try, I guess. "Umm, do you like Beyoncé?"

"Who doesn't?" Nic says, and Harper nods.

I type in "Countdown," one of the best Beyoncé songs

ever recorded. I hesitate before I hit play. Maybe I should start with one I don't like so much. I don't know if I can sing it in front of Harper and Nic.

"You can do it." Nic gives me a thumbs-up.

I take a deep breath and press play.

From the first trumpet notes, I know I'm not gonna be able to sit here and not sing. Nic's face lights up—she knows this one. Harper looks a little confused, but that's okay, it's not a really popular one.

Nic starts, her voice a rich, deep alto. Harper takes the phone to see the lyrics and mouths the words first, then sings in a slightly off-key mezzo-soprano. I move my shoulders to the beat, just a little. Noodle lifts her head. Nic and Harper are staring at the lyrics on Harper's phone and not at me. I can feel the trumpet in my bones.

When the second verse starts, I do too.

I close my eyes so I can't see them, and I sing as loud as I want. I start soft, but by the end of the song, I'm singing as loud as I would at home, when Dad's at work and Andrew's out.

When the song ends, I open my eyes. Nic and Harper are beaming at me.

"You did it!" Nic looks like she wants to hug me.

"My eyes were closed the whole time," I say sheepishly.

"Who cares? You sang in front of us without passing out." Harper grins at me. "Hundred percent improvement."

"Let's do another one! Avery, you pick."

We do a bunch of songs—"Crazy in Love," "Déjà Vu," the first part of "Before I Let Go." By the end of "Before I Let Go," we're all dancing and laughing and my chest is light and I don't feel panicked at all. I feel happy. Really and truly happy, for the first time since we moved.

We collapse on Nic's floor, giggling and out of breath. I'm breathing hard, but there's no panic attached. It's a miracle.

"Dang, Avery," Harper says, panting. "You about killed me with those high notes."

"Your range is unbelievable," Nic says. She looks at me, her brown eyes sparkling with something I can't name. "I could listen to you sing all day."

Well, *now* my heart's pounding. I have to look away, but I'm grinning uncontrollably.

"What do you want to do now?" Harper asks. "We know Avery can sing with the Queen, but I don't think we should do too much too fast."

"Agreed." I'm exhausted, and my throat is scratchy because I didn't warm up before yelling the lyrics to "Countdown" at the top of my lungs.

Nic sits up. She's got a mischievous gleam in her eyes. "Let's do sleepover stuff."

"Like sleep?" Harper grunts.

"Like truth or dare."

I sit up too, on high alert. Truth or dare never works out the way it does in movies. Someone's usually crying by the end of it. I would know. Andrew would too, after The Incident.

"Maybe we shouldn't do any dares," I say, twisting my shirt in my hands. "We don't want to make your mom mad at us."

"Okay, true." Nic still looks excited. It's almost like she's never played before. "Harper, are you okay with only truths?"

"I got nothing to hide," Harper says.

"Okay, it's settled! Who's going first?"

I don't like this idea. Harper may not have anything to hide, but I certainly do. There's Phantom, and the therapy thing, and I'd rather jump off a building than admit to Nic I like her. But I guess I could just lie about liking her, but then if I do tell her one day, she'll be like, "Why'd you lie to me that one time?" and that would be awkward—

"I'll go first." Harper sits up and looks at Nic. "Tell us why you were crying earlier."

Yikes. Harper's going straight for the neck. We could have warmed up first!

Nic's grin fades. "I was . . ." Nic trails off. I can practically see her trying to decide if she's going to lie or not. Finally, she sighs and slumps her shoulders. "Amberleigh said something really horrible to me today."

"What'd she say?" I ask. Despite fundamentally disagreeing with the concept of truth or dare, I am curious.

"We were talking about our siblings, and somehow we got on our brother's girlfriends. And Emily said her brother was dating a guy, and Amberleigh said that was disgusting."

"What a b—"

"Harper!"

"Sorry, sorry. Go ahead."

Nic smiles a little. "It was horrible. We got into a big fight because that's such a terrible thing to say. And Amberleigh just really . . . It just really made me mad. So now I guess we're not friends anymore."

Harper starts talking about how she shouldn't want to be Amberleigh's friend anyway because she seems like she's a jerk, but I'm thinking about Nic. Did she cry over what Amberleigh said, or did she cry because she and Amberleigh aren't friends anymore? I haven't told anyone I like girls (except Denny and now Andrew, somehow), and part of the reason is I'm not sure how people will react. I don't want anyone to hate me. Well, scratch that. I don't want *certain* people to hate me. Dad. Harper. Nic. Nic, especially.

But Nic said that what Amberleigh said was awful, so maybe she's an ally at least. Maybe she doesn't think I'm disgusting.

"Avery? Hello?" I look back at Harper, who's waving her hand in my face. "You still with us? It's your turn."

"Oh, uh . . ." I really want to ask Nic if she likes me, but I push that thought out of my mind. I could ask Harper about not going home, but maybe she doesn't want Nic to know. Or me. She seemed really upset, and she didn't call anyone to ask if she could stay over. "Okay, Harper—how'd you write the play? It's really good!"

Harper's expression turns thoughtful. "I don't really like plays, to be honest. I like novels. But Mrs. Wren told me about this modernizing Shakespeare contest, and I entered because there was a prize. Five grand."

"Whoa, really?"

Harper nods. "Really."

"Did you win?" Nic asks.

"Yep. I'm five K richer."

"Oh my God. You're rich!"

Harper laughs, but it's humorless and short. "No. They said I'm too young to claim it and put it in a bank account until I'm eighteen."

"That's still good though, isn't it?" I say. "You can use it for something cool later on."

Harper draws a circle in Nic's carpet. "I needed that money now. Not six years from now."

Nic and I exchange a worried look. Maybe I should have asked about her not going home after all.

"What would you use it for?" Nic asks.

Harper pauses for a long time. She stares down at her mismatched socks. "I'd run away."

I move closer to Harper, close enough to hold her hand if she wants. "You don't have to run away. You can stay with me anytime."

"Me too," Nic says quickly. "And you can talk to us about whatever, whenever."

Harper looks up. She's smiling, but her expression is

still a little sad. "Thanks, guys. Anyway, I'm done. Your turn, Nic."

Nic looks at me and I know she's gonna ask me a question. I try to curb my panic as Nic thinks. I'm sure it won't be bad. Surely she wouldn't ask if I liked her? I mean, I haven't been that obvious, surely—

"Okay, I got it," Nic says. "Avery, do you remember us talking at the beginning of the year?"

Oh no.

"And you talked to me about theater class?"

Please no.

"Why did you avoid me after that?"

I stare at Nic, my rising panic coming to a halt. "What?"

"You wouldn't talk to me after that. You even stopped riding the bus." Nic laughs a little, but it's tinged with uncertainty. "Did I say something wrong?"

I'm speechless. Early in the year, I completely humiliated myself. I've been obsessing over this conversation ever since, and she's right—I *did* stop talking to her after that. I remember it in painful detail: We were at the back of the lunch line. She asked me about how I liked theater class. I was stuttering, sweaty, and my hands were twitching. In fact, they were twitching so bad I dumped half of my McDonald's sweet tea on her and the other half on me. I ran away right after because I just knew Nic would think I was a weirdo. Plus, I'm sure I messed up her pretty yellow dress. I never saw her wear it again after that day.

And now Nic's saying she's sad I didn't talk to her?

"I . . ." I struggle for words. "I spilled my drink all over you, Nic."

"You what?" Harper says, leaning closer. "You're kidding."

"She's not kidding," Nic says, but she's laughing. "Ruined that horrible dress my mom bought me, so thank you!"

I just stare at her. She was . . . glad? "But I . . . Okay, even if you didn't mind the drink thing, I was a nervous wreck. I thought you'd think I was weird. And you wouldn't want to talk to me again."

"What? No way!" Nic's eyes grow round with shock. "I thought you were nice! And we talked about music and theater, so I thought we'd be good friends."

"Oh." That's all I can think of to say.

"Looks like you both misunderstood," Harper says. She's borderline laughing. "Avery, you get in your own way. Don't worry so much."

We move on from truth or dare to looking at our classmates' Instagrams, but Harper's words stick in my brain and won't let go. I get in my own way. Nic didn't think I was weird. She wasn't even mad about the tea thing, but I didn't know because I avoided her after that. I can sing in front of people, if it's Beyoncé and I'm with Harper and Nic.

Maybe I can do this play after all.

Chapter 24

I'm lying on Nic's floor in a tangle of blankets, but I'm wide awake. I'm almost too amped to sleep. Harper is on one side of me, in Nic's puffy purple sleeping bag, breathing deeply, and Nic is on the other, in another pile of blankets from her bed. She insisted on joining us on the floor. I can't believe I'm at a sleepover with Nic Pearson. She changed into cute pajama pants with ducks on them and a T-shirt, and a silk hat just like mine. Who knew Nic Pearson had duck pajamas? I look up at the faint stars painted on Nic's ceiling. Is this true happiness?

"Avery? Are you still awake?" Nic whispers.

I roll over to face her. "Yeah."

"Are you thinking about the play?"

Really I'm thinking about how it's good Nic can't see me in the dark because I'm overwhelmed with how close we are, but the play is there too. "Yeah."

"Don't worry, Avery. You've got this." I can just barely make out Nic's smile in the dark. "You did so great today! We'll have you singing in front of everyone in no time."

Yeah, right. Beyoncé in Nic's room is one thing. Juliet's songs in front of the whole school and Dad is another thing entirely.

"I see you don't believe me," Nic says. "When have I ever steered you wrong?"

Signing me up for this in the first place. But that would be mean to say out loud. "It's just kinda overwhelming. I wish you were Juliet."

I expect Nic to laugh, but she gets really quiet. Sweat beads pop out against my hairline. Was that the wrong thing to say?

"Can I tell you a secret?" Nic murmurs. I try to catch her eye in the dark, but I can barely see her.

My heart pounds against my ribs. "Yeah."

"I wish I was Juliet too."

I'm stunned by the quiet pain in her voice. She sounds close to tears. This has to hurt—Nic is a better actor than me in every way, but I got the part just because I can sing okay. It's not fair. Nic's not even a bad singer! She just can't hit high notes. "Well, you can have her if you want. We can talk to Mrs. Thompson on Monday."

"No, no! That's not it. I'm glad you're Juliet. Your voice is so pretty." Nic hesitates, and I know a "but" is coming. "But it just kinda sucks, you know? I'm always number two. Always. I'm the second sibling. I'm Amberleigh's second-favorite friend. Okay, well, zero favorite now probably, but you get it. And in elementary school, I was even the salutatorian. Like, I'm going crazy here. I'm always in second place. Everyone always remembers number one. Everyone forgets the second place." Nic takes a shaky breath. "I just thought, for this play, I could maybe be number one. Just one time."

Pressure builds behind my eyes. If I hadn't tried out, maybe she would have been Juliet. But she helped me and got punished for it. I reach for her hand this time and hang on tight when I find it.

"You're not number two to me."

There's a long silence, and then Nic bursts into quiet giggles.

"Avery, that was so corny."

"Sorry," I say, my face heating up. "But it's true! You were the first person to be nice to me since we moved. You were my first friend."

She squeezes my hand gently, and my face heats up more. Suddenly, I remember I'm lying on the floor of Nic's room, in the dark. Harper is dead asleep. Oh boy.

"Thank you for being my friend," Nic says, her voice soft. "And thanks for listening to my whining. I've never actually told anyone that before."

I'm burning up under these blankets. She trusts me enough to tell me something deep and personal . . . I'm overwhelmed. I wait too long to say something back, and Nic lets go of my hand.

"Okay, let's sleep. We got a lot of practice tomorrow!" Nic rolls over away from me, and her room fills with silence.

It takes me a few minutes to sort through the heated mush that is my brain. "Thank you for telling me."

She doesn't answer, so I think she's already asleep.

Chapter 25

"Okay, today we'll be acting out our parts!" Mrs. Thompson says on Monday, clapping her hands like it's the most exciting thing in the world. I immediately want to throw up, but fight past it. I can do it. I'm ready.

The sleepover was so much fun; we played games and watched movies until late Saturday, when Dad demanded I come home. Nic declared we should do one every week. Nic's mom shot that down right away, but I asked Dad if we can have one at my house this Friday, and he agreed. But he said we have to clean the whole house before they get there, so I spent all Sunday unpacking boxes. I finally found my sleeping bag.

I'm worried about Harper. She said she was okay to go

home on Sunday, but today she seemed really down. And she didn't bring lunch again. That's two weeks, at least. This is more than a we're-short-this-month thing, I think.

"Miss Williams, come on up." Mrs. Thompson motions for me to join her and the rest of the cast onstage. Nic gives me a reassuring thumbs-up.

I drag myself up the steps and take my place. Deep breaths. At first, Mrs. Thompson just wants us to practice exiting and entering the stage. I can do this. Emily is my cue person, and she signals for me to go. I feel a pang of longing. I wish me and Emily could switch places.

Then it's time to read our parts. The play opens with Romeo (Thomas) and Juliet (sadly, me) meeting in front of an apartment. Juliet is on a delivery for the donut shop and Romeo's passing by. I know the lines. Romeo's lines too, since Harper reads for Romeo in the mornings.

"From the top!" Mrs. Thompson calls from the bottom of the stage.

"Who do you work for? Alabaster's?" Thomas says.

"Yeah. What about you?" My voice is steady and strong,

because I'm imagining practicing with Nic and Harper. I know the lines. I can do it.

Thomas looks surprised. "I heard they had crappy donuts."

"Well, I heard Pona's Donuts were full of grease!"

I'm doing it. Line after line, I say them all with strength and only a little shakiness. Thomas says his lines perfectly too, getting really into character. I like Romeo a lot better than Thomas, so it's an improvement.

We go all the way until the first song, when Mrs. Thompson claps for us. "Miss Williams! Mr. Gage! You've done so well! Outstanding."

I'm beaming. Nic grins at me, and I can't stop feeling like I'm about to float away with happiness. I did it. I can avoid therapy, and Dad will be happy, and Nic might think I'm a little more impressive now, and she might even ask me on a date because she's so impressed—

"Now," Mrs. Thompson says, smiling at us, "let's sing."

All my happy feelings are gone in an instant.

Mrs. Thompson is saying something, but I'm hot all of a sudden. I did my lines, but I haven't tried singing in front of them yet. I don't think I can do it. I look to Nic and she mouths, "Don't panic." Easy for her to say.

"Ready?" Mrs. Thompson says, hovering over her laptop. No. No, not yet—

The first note to the first song plays over the speakers. I'm supposed to start, to sing about how Romeo and Juliet don't have to fight over donuts their parents make, but I can't make a sound. I know the words. I feel the music. But I look at the rest of the class watching me, listening, and I feel like I'm going to faint.

"Miss Williams, you missed your cue," Mrs. Thompson says, pausing the music.

I don't say anything, because I'm starting to get that shaky feeling before a panic attack.

"Miss Williams?" Mrs. Thompson prompts. I try to talk, but I'm onstage, really onstage, and in three weeks I'll be doing this for real, singing in front of everyone.

The world is getting those black spots in front of it. Suddenly, Nic appears at my side. She holds my hand, really tight.

"Hang on, Mrs. Thompson, we'll be right back." Nic drags me by the hand until we're backstage, away from everyone else. "Avery, are you having a panic attack?"

I nod, gasping. "I can't breathe."

Nic puts her hands on my shoulders, her face inches from mine. "Remember what you did at my house, okay? What can you touch?"

My jeans. My sweaty script. Nic's hands on my shoulders.

"Better?" Nic asks tentatively.

Not yet. My lungs are still tight, barely letting any air in. I squeeze my eyes closed. When the touch thing doesn't work, I have to distract myself. I have a math test tomorrow, and I haven't studied. My lungs get tighter. Oops, wrong thing to think about. Okay, I brought a hairbrush for Phantom today. I've gotta comb out her fur. Phantom's face pops in my mind, and I imagine holding her, singing to her, and slowly I feel a bit better.

When I can take shallow, wheezy breaths, I open my eyes. Nic's watching me anxiously. "You okay?"

"Y-yeah." I'm shaking all over. I hold my hands together, trying to steady them.

"Let's sit down." Nic sits against the wall—close to Phantom's closet. I sit in front of the door, so she doesn't think to open it. Nic sits next to me while I control my breathing, until it's back to normal. But my heart is still racing and I'm still shaking.

"That was a bad one, huh?" Nic meets my eyes, hers sympathetic.

"Yeah. A real bad one."

Nic blows out a breath. "It's okay. We'll get through this, I promise. You did so well with your lines today, so we just gotta figure out how to get you to sing. Maybe Mrs. Thompson will let us do private practice?"

"Until when?" I can't keep the misery out of my voice. "I have to sing eventually. In front of everyone—" My voice hitches, and I can feel the tears coming. I turn away so Nic won't see.

Nic is quiet for a few minutes while I try to stop crying.

Then she says, "I'm sorry, Avery." Her voice is quiet and pained.

"It's okay. It's not your fault." I take a deep breath. Come on, Avery. Get it together. I turn back to Nic and smile. "Can we sit here until class is over, you think?"

"Definitely." Nic scoots closer to me, and we sit in silence, listening to the class practice the play without us.

Chapter 26

After theater, I don't visit Phantom. Instead, I run home and up the stairs and collapse on my bed so I can finish crying.

I was doing really well. I practiced. I almost have my lines memorized. I even know the songs. But I can't sing in front of everyone. The play is in three weeks. What am I going to do?

I google "how to cure anxiety" on my phone. Get more exercise, get more sleep, quit smoking. Pretty sure I'm okay on the smoking part, and I do sleep a lot and PE counts as exercise. But I still have panic attacks. I start to feel even worse. Then I see it—counseling. Therapy. That brings more tears to my eyes. I don't want therapy. I want to be able to handle this on my own. I want to be normal.

A notification pops up over Google. A text from Nic: *are you okay?*

I turn my phone over and bury my face in my pillow. I don't want to talk to her right now. There's a first time for everything, I guess.

I hear Andrew's shoes tromping upstairs, but I can't stop myself from sobbing into my pillow. This play is a nightmare I can't wake up from. I know the music . . . right? As a test, I sing all four of the play's songs from memory, softly, my voice broken and shaky from crying. The third song is a little off-key, and I forgot a few of the lyrics on the second one, but I can do it. I can sing. I know the words, the notes, even the little dance at the end. But I can't do it in front of anyone.

If I can't figure out how to sing onstage, all my, and Nic's and Harper's, hard work is worthless. And it'll be all my fault.

* * *

The next day, after another disastrous theater class—Mrs. Thompson doesn't even *try* to get me to sing, I was so awful the day before—I visit Phantom. I'm petting her back and feeling sorry for myself when my phone rings.

It's Andrew.

I stare at my phone in shock. Andrew has never called me before. Is everything okay? Is Dad hurt?! Phantom looks up at me from my lap, tilting her head to one side. I answer the phone with shaky hands.

"H-hello?"

"Nothing's wrong," Andrew says. My shoulders immediately relax. "Are you at school still?"

"Yeah . . . why?"

"I'm gonna pick you up. Be out front in ten minutes." Before I can say anything, he hangs up.

What's that about? He's never picked me up from school before. I don't get Andrew at all. I look down at Phantom. "Why are brothers so weird?"

Phantom closes her eyes and purrs. She probably doesn't know either.

I wait eight minutes before putting Phantom back in her bed. I kiss the top of her head. "Bye! Love you. I'll bring you *two* sandwiches tomorrow! But you can't tell Harper." Harper thinks she's too fat and needs to go on a diet. I think she's perfect and should get all the treats she wants.

I close Phantom's door and leave the theater to go to the front. I look around for Harper, but I don't see her. She doesn't hang out with me every day after school. I wonder where she goes. She doesn't seem to like her house very much.

Andrew's standing at the front with his hands in his jacket pockets. "You're late," he grunts when I get closer.

"I'm not. You said ten minutes." I adjust the straps on my backpack. "What do you want?"

"Ice cream," he says. And then he starts walking away.

I hurry to catch up, completely confused. "Ice cream? What? Where? Why?"

"I just wanted some," he says, not looking at me. "Didn't want to go by myself."

I walk behind him for a minute, thinking. Maybe Andrew

wants to talk about something? Now that I think about it, Andrew hasn't hung out with anyone lately. He's just been moping at home. I catch up with him and walk beside him. "It's okay, Andrew. I know you don't have friends here yet. I'm here to listen."

Andrew looks down at me and makes an ugly face. "Wow, you get two friends and now you think you're big time." He rolls his eyes. "And I don't have anything to talk about."

"Then why are we getting ice cream?" I press. I don't even know where we're going. All the good ice cream places are too far to walk to.

"Geez, Avery, you talk too much. Just be grateful I'm buying."

I don't say anything. Andrew really is weird. I bet Dad told him to hang out with me, and he's just not good at it.

I follow Andrew in silence for a few minutes, but I don't have to wait long. Two big yellow arches appear in the distance. Well, there's worse ice cream than McDonald's.

When we get inside, Andrew tells me to pick a seat. He

comes back a few minutes later with two Oreo McFlurries. "When did ice cream get so expensive?" he mutters.

"Thanks." I take a few bites. It's unbearably sweet. I want three of them.

"So . . ." Andrew says, wolfing down his own ice cream. "Do you want to talk about something?"

I knew it. A trap. "No. Did Dad tell you to ask me?"

"Dad didn't hear you crying your eyes out last night."

I wince. He heard me. I knew he was home, but I didn't think he'd hear me . . . or even care if he did.

"Well?" Andrew says. He's almost done with his McFlurry.

I draw a circle in my ice cream with my spoon. I didn't want to talk to Nic and Harper about it, but Andrew doesn't know anything about theater. Maybe it's safe to talk about with him. "I can't sing onstage."

"You've got some time, don't you?"

"Yeah, but what if I still can't do it when the play comes—"

"Don't worry about that yet," he says. He tosses his empty

cup in the trash can behind him. "You've got three weeks. Chill, Avery."

"I can't chill," I snap. "I have anxiety."

Andrew laughs a little. "Yeah, sorry. But anyway, don't worry about it until it's really a problem. Like a week before or whatever."

I guess he's right. Theater was kind of terrible today, but I really nailed my lines. So I am getting better. Maybe I'll be able to do it before the play. "Okay. Thanks, Andrew."

Andrew nods. "Is that all? Just the play?"

I scratch at the table. I'm not really hungry anymore. "Well . . . Dad said I might have to go to therapy."

"I heard," Andrew says. "What do you think?"

"I don't want to go." My words are rushed. "Everyone will think I'm weird and it costs a lot of money and Dad will have to take off from work to take me—"

Andrew holds his hands up. "Okay, okay, slow down. Forget about the logistics. We'll handle that if it comes. Think about just the therapy itself. Do you think it'll help your anxiety?"

I struggle for words. I don't know; I've never been. I end up just shrugging.

Andrew sighs. "All right, just think about it. Talk to your new friends when they invade the house on Friday. But I can't keep buying you ice cream. This junk is expensive."

I smile into my cup. I don't know what changed with Andrew, but he's not such a jerk anymore. It's almost like before we moved. I dig my spoon into the too-sweet ice cream again.

"Thanks, Andrew. I will."

Chapter 27

"Hurry, Avery," Dad yells over the vacuum. "They'll be here any minute!"

I dump the boxes from last night's dinner in the trash. It's Friday, and Nic and Harper are coming over soon. Dad's freaking out more than I am. He keeps muttering, "We live in a pigpen," and vacuuming the living room. We already unpacked all the boxes, finally, so it doesn't look too bad. But I guess Dad is nervous to have guests. No one ever came to our tiny apartment.

The doorbell rings. I race to get it before Andrew can answer and embarrass me.

I open the door and reveal both Nic and Harper. Nic has

a huge duffel bag and her sleeping bag, but Harper's just got a Walmart bag. They both grin when they see me.

"Party time!" Nic says, holding up her stuff.

I let them in and take them to the kitchen. "Dad, this is Harper and Nic. Well, you know Nic."

"Hey, Mr. Williams!" Nic's beaming. "I love your house. It's so cool."

"Hi, Mr. Williams," Harper says, nodding awkwardly.

Dad smiles at them. "Hi, girls. I'm glad you're here. Avery doesn't have many friends, so—"

"We're going to my room!" I say loudly as Andrew snickers on the couch.

"When you get hungry, come down! We'll order pizza."

"Okay, bye, Dad, love you!" I hurry Nic and Harper upstairs before he can accidentally embarrass me again.

Nic and Harper put their stuff down, and I close the door behind us. "Sorry, my dad is too much."

"He's really cool," Nic says.

"He's really tall," Harper says. "I thought I was gonna break my neck."

"And yet, I'm four eleven."

Nic and Harper laugh, and I can't help grinning. It's so much easier to talk to them now than it was before. I don't know what changed, but I hope this lasts forever.

We practice for the play. When it's time to sing, I get a little nervous, but I channel the Beyoncé marathon and get through the songs okay. It helps that Harper likes to sing loudly and also the wrong notes, so I'm mostly laugh-singing.

Dad orders us pizza, and we watch a movie. It's fun, and more than that, I don't feel nervous at all. Even when Nic leans against me to show me something on her phone or asks me who my favorite artist is besides Beyoncé (Ariana Grande, of course, in more ways than one). By the time it's bedtime, I'm in a great mood. My room is smaller than Nic's, so I have to sleep in my bed while Harper and Nic are on the floor.

"Night, Avery!" Nic says cheerfully. Harper's already rolled over onto her side. She waves at us but doesn't say anything.

"Good night." I think about what Andrew said, about asking them about therapy, but I reject the idea. I don't need to ask them. I don't want to go. That's just it. "See you tomorrow."

I'm drifting off when Harper calls my name.

"Yes?" I whisper back. Nic is asleep—I know because she's snoring! It's really cute. She said she thought she was catching a cold, and I guess this proves it.

"Are you sleepy?"

Yes, but something in Harper's tone makes me pause. "No, what's up?"

"Can we talk?"

I sit up in bed. "Yeah. Let's go downstairs so we don't wake Nic up."

We tiptoe carefully around Nic and go downstairs to the kitchen. Harper looks tired, like she hasn't slept in a while. Dark bruises stain the skin under her eyes.

"Do you want some more pizza?" I offer. She always eats like she's starving. Which is good, because lately I've been too anxious to eat. Today's the first day I had a full meal in a week.

Harper shakes her head. "No. Thanks though."

I get us two bottles of water from the fridge anyway and sit across from Harper at the table. I wait for her to speak, but she just picks at the table.

"Umm . . . what'd you want to talk about?"

Harper looks up at me. "Can I ask you something really personal?"

Oh boy. I think fleetingly of Nic snoring upstairs. "Y-yeah. Go for it."

"What happened to your mom?"

The question sucks all the air out of my lungs. I haven't thought about her in a long time. Since Mother's Day last year, maybe.

Harper's serious expression melts into an anxious one. "Oh God, she's dead, isn't she? I'm so sorry. I shouldn't have asked."

"No, umm, it's okay. She's not dead." I try to figure out

how I'm gonna tell this story. No one has asked me in a while. "Well, before me, there was just Dad, and Andrew, and her. They fought a lot because I guess she didn't like being a mom. Then I came. And they fought more. She left me one day at day care and never came back."

Harper's face is full of pity, which kinda makes me mad. She asked. "I'm sorry, Avery."

"It's okay, really. I can't remember her. It's just me and Dad and Andrew. That's how it's always been." I fiddle with my water bottle, the thought of her bringing my mood down. "I think Andrew used to hate me for it though. Like he thought I was the reason she left. I don't know if he's right. I can't remember."

"You weren't the reason." Harper looks into my eyes. "Trust me."

The "trust me" reminds me that Harper wanted to talk. "Why'd you ask? I don't mind. I just wondered why now?"

It's Harper's turn to mess with her water bottle. "I just wanted to know, because I thought I could ask your advice. But I guess your mom is a little different."

"What do you mean?"

"There's something I haven't told you. You can't tell anyone else."

"Okay. I promise." My heart beats faster, but I try to stay calm for Harper.

Harper takes a deep breath. "Sometimes I think my mom doesn't like me very much."

"What do you mean?"

"I don't know. She gets really mad at me sometimes over stupid stuff." Harper seems angry now, clutching her water bottle in a tight fist. "She screamed at me because Mrs. Corrie told her I got a C on my math test. But that was a really hard test! And I did okay on the other ones."

It *was* a hard test. I got a C too. "Maybe she's really stressed? Andrew gets like that when he's upset."

"Maybe . . ." Harper glances down at her cup. "I don't know. I just kinda started noticing it."

"Noticing what?"

"Like, your dad is really cool. And he's really nice to you. And Nic's mom and dad are nice to her too. Even if Nic's mom acts mad that she didn't ask before we came over, she's not *really* mad. Not the kind of mad I've seen."

This sounds bad. Really bad. I remember Harper not wanting to go home. "Umm, can I ask you something personal too?"

Harper nods.

"Are you . . . okay? With your mom? Like, safe?"

Harper's eyes fill with tears. "It's not like she hits me or anything."

"But?"

"But . . ." Harper sniffles, and she's really crying now. "But she treats me like she hates me. She's always yelling at me or just doesn't come home. I wish I could just stay with my aunt. I wish they'd just give me my stupid five K so I could get out of here."

I get up and hug Harper. She clings to me, sobbing on my shoulder, and I hold her as tight as I can because I'm crying now too. This is horrible. Harper doesn't deserve this.

When we're just sniffling, I pull away. I put my hands on Harper's shoulders, like Nic did for me. "It's okay. We're gonna figure this out. We have a guest room, so you can stay with me whenever you want."

Harper wipes her eyes on her pajama shirt. "Thanks, Avery. Sorry I cried. That's so embarrassing."

"I cry at least twice a week over the play, so you're good." I give her a smile, and she smiles back.

"Thanks for letting me vent. I feel better."

"What're friends for?"

Harper laughs and wipes her eyes again. "Best friends at this point, I think."

We go back to my room and lie down, but I can't shake the warm feeling Harper's words gave me. But I also can't get the image of Harper crying out of my mind. I have to do something. This is way bigger than therapy. I gotta figure out how to help her. I close my eyes, my chest full of happiness and dread.

Chapter 28

I slam down my last card in UNO. "I win!!"

Harper groans, and Andrew swears, tossing his card to the table. "That's the last time I let you nerds win," Andrew says, standing and stretching. I grin up at him as he stalks out of the room. He's always been a sore loser.

It's Sunday night, and Harper stayed with me an extra night after the sleepover ended. Dad didn't seem to mind, which is great because I love having Harper around. She teams up with me against Andrew, and she loves watching movies and it's been so much fun. We sang together again (Harper wasn't knowledgeable about Beyoncé's greatest songs, but I fixed that) and looked for some toys for

Phantom. I wish she could just live with us. I've always wanted a sister.

Harper cleans up the cards, shaking her head. "I don't know how you're so good at this. How can someone win all three rounds?"

"It helps when you have Andrew to practice against. He's terrible at games and he hates losing, so it's fun."

Harper laughs. "I bet Nic could beat us both into the ground. She has three brothers to practice with."

"Oh yeah, definitely."

Harper looks up at me, and I pause. She's grinning, but it's a sly, mischievous one. Uh oh.

"So, speaking of Nic . . ." Harper casually puts the cards back in the UNO box. "I was wondering if you liked her."

I feel like I've been punched in the gut. This can't be happening! First Andrew, now Harper?! Am I that obvious?!

"I won't tell her," Harper assures me. "I've just been meaning to ask you."

"How . . . ?" I can barely talk. I'm burning up. I need some water. "How'd you know?"

"Oh, I don't know, the way you look at her, the way you get excited when she talks to you, the way you're killing yourself to do this play just because she asked you to . . ." Harper grins at me. "Just a few things."

I slump against the couch. So I really *am* that obvious. Twelve years of hiding my secret has done me no good.

"Okay, fine. Yes. I do like her." It feels kinda good to say it out loud. "But you can't tell her, Harper. Please. You have to promise."

"I promise. But you know, I think she wouldn't care. She might even like you too!"

I snort. Yeah, right. What's there to like? I'm an anxious, sweaty mess. And she probably doesn't even like girls. "I can't risk telling her. What if she hates me?"

"I don't think that'd happen. But I get it." Harper pats my arm sympathetically. "I won't say anything, but you should tell her eventually. You might be surprised."

Harper's looking right into my eyes. What does she

mean I "might be surprised"? Surprised that Nic won't mind? Or . . .

Dad interrupts my thoughts by coming out of the kitchen. "Girls, it's getting late. Let me take you home, Harper."

Harper deflates like a balloon. Her shoulders slump, and her head hangs low. "Okay, Mr. Williams."

"Can she stay another night? Please?" I try to use my best begging expression, but Dad shakes his head.

"It's a school night. But you're welcome to come back next weekend."

Harper goes upstairs to get her stuff from my room, but I stay with Dad. "Come on, Dad," I say, my voice low. "She looks so sad."

"She can't stay forever. And you'll see her at school."

That's not it at all, but I don't get a chance to explain. Harper comes downstairs with her bag, and Dad ushers us out of the house. When we're both buckled into the back seat, Dad turns around to face us. "Where to, Harper?"

"I live close to Dairy Queen," she says. "Oh, wait, do you know where that is? I forgot you just moved here."

No, we know where it is, and it's really far away! At least a twenty-minute walk. And she walks to school every day?

Dad doesn't notice my alarm. He says, "I know where that is! Taxi service is headed out." He pulls out of the driveway, and we're on the way.

Harper doesn't say anything the whole ride, and I feel bad breaking her concentration. She looks like she's deep in thought. When we get close to Dairy Queen, she gives Dad directions, and soon we're outside an apartment complex. It looks a lot like our old one, with creaky black railings and peeling paint on the sides. But hers also has a fenced-in pool! It's tiny, but that's pretty cool. I wonder if she'd let me and Nic swim with her in the summer.

"Well, this is it." Harper gathers her stuff. She looks at me. "See you tomorrow."

"Okay. See you tomorrow." Harper gets out of the car and closes the door behind her. I poke my head out the window and wave. "You can come over again next weekend!"

Harper smiles and waves back, but doesn't say anything. Dad and I watch her climb three flights of steps and unlock the fourth door from the right. Dad waits until she's inside before he cranks up the car again.

"So . . ." Dad trails off as we leave Harper's neighborhood. "About Harper."

"Yeah?"

I can't see Dad's face, but I imagine him frowning at the road. "She didn't seem very happy to go home."

"No, she's not." I sigh, thinking of her crying on my shoulder Friday night.

"Do you know what's going on?"

"Kinda. But you can't tell anyone." Dad nods, and I continue. "She doesn't like her mom that much."

"What do you mean? Like she's hard on her?"

"Yeah, kinda." I think about what Harper said Friday night. "She says she feels kinda lonely, but I don't think that's it. She never brings lunch to school. And she seems really sad all the time."

"Hmm." Dad taps his finger on the steering wheel but doesn't say anything.

"Hmm what?"

"Nothing. Just thinking." Dad glances at me in the rear-view mirror. "Don't worry about it, Avery. She'll be okay."

I cross my arms. Easy for him to say. I can't help but worry about her; she's my friend. Maybe Dad will let her stay over more often. I'll have to ask him later. I look out the window, trying to think about a plan of attack to convince Dad to temporarily adopt Harper, but Harper's sad face remains front of mind.

Chapter 29

"I can't believe they're making us choose." Thomas is practically glaring at me.

"It's not fair." I take a shaky breath. I'm already trembling and sweaty. Today we have to sing, and the cue for the second song is coming up. "What can we do? We have to listen to our parents."

"We can run away." Thomas looks at me, his eyebrows raised. I'm supposed to sing the first note of the second song now. I open my mouth to sing.

Nothing comes out.

Thomas throws his hands up in the air. "I can't do this," he says. "Why are we even trying? She'll never be able to sing onstage."

"You better watch it, Thomas," Nic says, coming to stand beside me. She puts her hands on her hips and stands taller. "Avery's doing fine. Just needs a little more practice."

"Says who? The play's in less than two weeks!"

My stomach sinks when the other actors exchange glances and start nodding. Thomas is right. I can't do this. I'm dragging everyone down. I—

"We just need more practice." Nic looks irritated, but I hope it's not at me. I hope it's not because she agrees with him.

"Practice isn't gonna make a mute sing."

"Oh, really? Well, practice won't fix your tone-deaf singing either!"

"Okay, enough." Mrs. Thompson climbs onstage before Nic and Thomas can get into a fistfight. Thomas's face is red up to his hairline. "Mr. Gage, take a few minutes to cool off. Miss Pearson, you too." Mrs. Thompson locks eyes with me. "Miss Williams, come to my office."

Humiliation threatens to drown me as I follow Mrs.

Thompson to her office. This is it. She's gonna fire me from my first acting role. This is terrible. Worst-case scenario.

"Take a seat, Miss Williams." Mrs. Thompson sits at her desk, and I sit on one of the stools she has scattered in her office. She folds her hands and watches me. She doesn't seem mad or even disappointed. "Sing the second song for me."

I stare at her, in shock. "Right now?"

"Right now."

"Without music?" Mrs. Thompson nods. Oh God, okay. I clear my throat, close my eyes, and sing. I know all the words now. Even the middle lyrics don't trip me up. I think I even keep on tempo without the accompaniment. When I stop, I open my eyes. Mrs. Thompson is smiling, so maybe I did a good job.

"You've been practicing."

I nod, not trusting my voice. At least she doesn't think I've just been slacking off. I've been trying really hard. I just can't do it.

"Why did you try out for this play, Miss Williams?"

I look to the floor. Because Nic wanted me to. Because I thought it would make Dad happy. Because I like to sing. Just not like this. "I—I wanted to."

Mrs. Thompson nods to herself. "Well, Miss Williams, I think you can do this, if it's what you want. But *you* have to want it. Not because your friend wants it for you. Do you understand?"

I nod, afraid to speak. I might start crying.

"I have faith in you, Miss Williams. We all get stage fright. It's just about how you personally deal with it. Just think about it."

The bell rings, ending the school day. Mrs. Thompson smiles at me, but I can't find the energy to smile back. I'm still Juliet, and I still can't sing onstage. I can't give up now, especially since Dad will wonder why I quit and cart me off to therapy. Nic defended me, and Harper's been helping me practice too. Everyone is depending on me to nail this. But I don't know if I can do it, and that fact makes me want to throw up.

Chapter 30

I head to the theater to bring Phantom her sandwich, feeling low.

It's been a few days since Thomas blew up at me. I've been practicing really hard. I made Andrew sit in my room, and I sang all four songs to him. I even had my eyes open! But I still can't do it. No matter how hard I try, I can't sing in class. It's seven days until Valentine's Day. Seven days between me and disaster.

Phantom meows loudly when I open her closet door, pawing at my shoelaces. I pick her up, and she starts purring.

"Phantom, just sing for me. I bet people would love it."

Phantom responds by pawing at my backpack. I guess we can talk after lunch is served.

I put her down and pull out the turkey sandwich. She gobbles down the meat greedily. I put away the leftover bread. I don't think I can eat it. I haven't felt like eating this whole week.

"Okay, now back to business, Phantom. What am I gonna do? I have a week to figure everything out. That's not a lot of time, and I—"

"Avery?"

Harper's voice calls me from the front of the stage. She's earlier than usual. I hastily put Phantom's toy back, and she climbs onto her cat bed.

"Don't worry," I say, scratching behind her ears. "I'll be back after school, promise."

I go to the front of the stage, where Harper's waiting on me. Nic has been joining us for lunch lately, but she's not here yet.

"Hey, sorry, I was just—"

"What did you do?"

I freeze. Harper's face is red—she's been crying. But worse than that, she looks mad. Really mad.

"What? I didn't—"

"Who did you tell?" Harper's voice is cracking, but I can't tell if it's from fury or if she's about to cry.

"Tell what?" Panic reaches its claws into my throat. She's mad at me, but I don't know why. "I don't understand—"

"I know you told someone about me and my mom!" Harper's yelling now, her face bright red.

Nic enters the theater, but I barely notice her coming in. "I didn't tell anyone, I swear."

"Then why did Mom yell at me?" Harper's still yelling, but she's crying too. "Someone called, and then after that she started screaming at me. She said since I'm so unhappy, I can get out. Where am I supposed to go?!"

I don't know what to say. I didn't tell anyone. And I mean, she has been staying at our house a lot, but I don't think that matters. Who would even know—

Dad. He asked me about Harper. Oh God.

"Harper . . ." I try to find the words to apologize, but Harper turns around and storms out of the theater.

Nic looks between Harper and me, her expression

anxious. Before she can say anything, I run to the back of the stage. I open Phantom's closet—she blinks sleepily against the light. I pull the door closed before Nic can follow me, sink to the floor, and burst into tears.

Phantom crawls into my lap, and I hug her tight. This is my fault. I didn't even think to lie when Dad asked me. Harper trusted me. Harper called me her best friend. And I ruined everything.

I hug Phantom and cry all through lunch, but for once, her purring doesn't make me feel any better.

Chapter 31

"You're awful quiet tonight," Dad says at dinner.

I push around the carrots on my plate and don't answer. I don't know what to say to him. How could he get Harper in trouble? Why did he do it? Harper can just stay with us until things calm down. I don't get it.

Nic texted me and said she talked to Harper after our fight. Harper's staying with her aunt, which is a big relief. Harper likes her aunt a lot. And luckily she doesn't live far away. But when I texted her and apologized, she didn't answer.

"Is everything okay?" Dad asks, his tone unsure.

I push away from the table. "I'm going to my room."

"Avery, wait." Dad sighs heavily. "We need to talk."

"Yeah, we do." At least he's gonna come clean about it. I cross my arms and wait.

Dad hesitates for a second. "Do you remember what I said about therapy?"

No. No, this can't be happening.

"Mrs. Thompson told me you've been having panic attacks again. And you haven't been eating much." Dad breathes out heavily. "I just think this is the next step. I booked an appointment for you. After the play."

There's a high-pitched buzzing in my ears. I feel like I'm about to pass out. It's like a panic attack is coming, but I don't feel panicked. I'm mad.

"Uh oh," Andrew mutters from across the table.

"This isn't fair!" I'm on my feet now, shaking with rage. "You promised me! You promised you'd let me handle it!"

"Avery—"

"Why do you always get to do whatever you want? I had to move here and everyone hates me and Andrew's a jerk—"

"Hey—"

"—and you went and told on Harper, and now she's really

mad at me and doesn't want to be my friend anymore. And now you're gonna make me go to stupid therapy and everyone will think I'm a bigger freak than they already do! This sucks."

"Hey," Dad says, his voice carrying a warning. "I know you're upset, but don't use that word. We'll get through this—"

"I don't care!" I'm screaming at him now. I worked so hard on this stupid play, all for him, all so he wouldn't worry about me, and it doesn't even matter. "The only thing you care about is your stupid job now. Well, I hate that job and I hate you!"

I run upstairs, my chest about to burst, and slam my door. Dad calls me and tries to talk to me through the door, but I put in my earphones and drown him out with music. I hug my legs, my face pressed against my knees, and cry until I don't have anything left.

"I love you, Juliet," Thomas says. He's in his costume now, and so am I. Dress rehearsal. The play is four days away.

"I love you too." I can hear my voice is flat, but I don't care. I'm not in the mood for this.

Harper hasn't been back to school. She's not answering any of my texts. I haven't talked to Dad either. He keeps trying, but I'm so mad at him. I'm so mad at everyone. I don't want to practice right now. Everything's fallen apart, and this dumb play is at the center.

"You could at least pretend to care," Thomas says, frustration in his tone.

"Mr. Gage," Mrs. Thompson warns. "Let's try again. One more time, Miss Williams."

I don't want to do this one more time. Nic gives me a sympathetic thumbs-up. We have a scene together after this, so if I can just get through Thomas's scene, I'll be okay.

I take a deep breath. Just a little more. "I love you too! But we can't be together. Mom will never let us."

"Meet me at the train station at eleven tonight. We'll run away, and that'll show them."

"Love is more important than donuts." Debatable. I'm gonna have to ask Harper about that line. Well, I would if she ever wanted to talk to me again.

Thomas's face screws up with disgust. "You're not even trying."

Something in me snaps. I rear back and throw my script at Thomas. It hits him in the head. "You do it, then!" I scream as he howls in pain. "If you're so perfect, play both parts! Good luck kissing yourself, you jerk!"

The theater is silent as I stomp down the steps and out of the building. I'm too mad to cry. I just have to get out of here.

I end up at the playground by my house. It's empty except for a lady reading a book on a bench. I sit on the swing, my stomach swirling with anxiety and regret. I bet Thomas will hate me now. Well, more than he does already. Maybe I'll even be suspended. My stomach clenches so hard I want to throw up. Dad will have to stay at home from work if I'm suspended. He'll be so mad at me.

Wait, why do I care? I'm mad at him. I'm glad he'll have to leave that dumb suit job to watch me. I try to muster the anger again, the rage that flared up at Thomas, but tears well up in my eyes instead.

"I thought you'd be here."

I look up at Nic. She's smiling at me, but her expression is worried too. For some reason, that irritates me. I don't feel like talking to anyone right now.

Nic sits in the swing next to me. "Thomas is gonna have a bruise for sure. You really nailed him. Serves him right though. I don't like him either."

I draw a circle in the sand with the toe of my shoe. "Do you think I'll get in trouble?"

"Nah. He was taunting you." Nic hesitates. "But you might get in trouble for skipping school. I thought you were gonna come back, but you didn't."

I shrug. "I didn't want to."

Nic meets my eyes. "I'm sorry about Harper, Avery. I know that's bothering you."

I don't say anything. I don't want to talk about it.

"But if it helps, I think you did the right thing," Nic says. "I was kinda worried about her too—"

"I didn't tell on her!" Frustration bubbles out of my mouth into a scream. "Dad did. Even though I told him he couldn't tell anyone."

"Sorry," Nic says quickly. "We can talk about something else."

I don't want to talk. I stand up out of the swing. "I'm going home."

"Wait, Avery." Nic stands too, concern all over her face. "I know you're stressed out about Harper and the play, but maybe we can talk? You've been really quiet, and the thing with Thomas . . . I'm worried about you."

I look at Nic, at her cute freckles and how pretty her eyes are, and the anger bubbles up again. This is all her fault. I never would have met Harper or her if she hadn't pushed me into singing.

"Go away!" I'm crying now, and I can't stop. "Just leave me alone! This is all your fault. I never wanted to be Juliet. I hate this play, and I just want to go home. Leave me alone."

I turn away from Nic and run home so I don't have to look at her heartbroken face.

Chapter 32

There's a knock at my door.

I'm lying facedown on my bed. I turn my head to the side, exhausted. "Go away, Dad."

"Not Dad."

I sit up a little. Andrew? What does he want?

"Can I come in?"

I lie back down. "Sure."

Andrew opens my door. He stands next to my bed, shaking his head. "Man, you look terrible."

"I changed my mind. You can leave."

Andrew laughs and sits on the floor beside my bed. "So, heard you escaped from school. Pretty hard core."

So the school called Dad? I close my burning eyes.

"You didn't come to dinner again," Andrew continues. "Third day in a row."

"I'm not hungry."

"Yeah, I know. You get like this when your anxiety's bad." Andrew leans against my bed, his long legs stretched out. "You want to talk it out?"

I didn't before, but I'm not so mad anymore. I'm just sad. This is the worst day of my life. Worse than the day Nic caught me singing, or when I embarrassed myself the first time I talked to Harper. I lost everything: Nic, Harper, Dad. And I *still* have to sing in front of everyone. It's unbearable.

"I messed up, Andrew." My voice is quiet. "My friends are mad at me."

"Wow. You just made them too."

I hit Andrew in the head with my pillow, but my heart's not in it. He's right. It's not Nic's fault. I ruined everything.

"Your friends'll come back. And if they don't, you'll make new ones. You'll be okay. Now, about this play."

"What about it?"

"It's making you miserable." Andrew says it like it's a fact.

It's not even a question. "Why'd you try out if you didn't want to do it?"

"I did want to do it. Just not the biggest part, you know? And I didn't want Dad to worry about me. I thought if I did the play, he'd think I was doing better."

"Do you think he's not worried now? You haven't eaten dinner in three days. You ran away from school. We can hear you crying up here, you know."

My eyes well up with tears. I ruined everything. Even not making Dad worry. "What should I do, Andrew? The play is Friday. I still can't sing onstage."

"That's up to you, little sis." Andrew gets to his feet. He pats my head, his touch uncommonly gentle. "By the way, I'll come to your dumb play. So you've got one fan."

"Really?"

"Really." Andrew messes up my hair before leaving the room. "Good luck deciding what to do. You've got this."

I watch Andrew leave my room, a hollow pit that has nothing to do with hunger in my stomach. Up to me. I close my eyes. I wish I knew what to do.

Chapter 33

I peek into the lunchroom cautiously. I don't see Nic anywhere, thank goodness. I don't know what I'd say. I check the edge of the cafeteria, and I freeze.

Harper.

She's sitting where I first saw her, her head down. There's a brown paper bag in front of her—she has a lunch today! I want to talk to her, to apologize, but my heart is in my throat and I'm having trouble breathing. Maybe I can catch her after school. Maybe she'll meet me in the theater, like she used to.

I leave the lunchroom and head to the theater. I need to see Phantom. If I can hold her, just for a few minutes, I'll be calmer and I can talk to Harper and Nic and apologize.

That's what I've decided to do. Andrew is right—it's up to me.

I go outside to the theater, but I hear someone running after me. I look back, curious, and my heart skips a beat—it's Nic.

"Avery! Avery, wait." Nic catches up to me, panting.

I'm too nervous to speak. I didn't think I'd see her so soon. The "I'm sorry" is right on the tip of my tongue, but I can't say it.

"I know you're mad at me, but I have something to show you." Nic's face is really serious. "I think it'll help you feel better."

Oh God, I have no idea what she's going to show me. I nod, and she leads me to the theater. It's empty, as usual. I look at our normal eating spot forlornly. I wish Harper was here.

"Wait here," Nic says. She pulls out her phone and sends a rapid text. "I'm gonna show Harper too."

My heart rate kicks up. "Nic—"

"It's okay! I promise she's not mad anymore." Nic's easy

confidence helps slow my heart a bit, but I'm still nervous. Harper seemed so angry . . .

We wait for a few minutes, and soon the theater door opens. Harper peeks in cautiously. We make eye contact, but I look at the floor. I can't do this. I don't want her to be mad at me. I can't take it along with everything else.

"Come on, come on," Nic says, ushering Harper closer. "You're both gonna love this, I swear. Hurry, but be quiet."

What on earth is Nic going to show us? She leads us up the stage steps, then past the curtain, to the back . . . and stands by Phantom's closet. My eyes widen as Nic throws open the door and Phantom blinks at us.

"Look! I found a cat back here!"

I look at Phantom, then Harper. And then I just start laughing. All the stress and worry and pain are gone. Nic found a cat—my cat—and the first thing she thought was to come and show me. Even after I said something terrible to her. It's all so absurd. I'm laughing so hard tears come from my eyes. I can't breathe. I can't believe this. Harper starts laughing too, and I pick up Phantom and hold her to my chest.

"Nic," I wheeze, barely able to hold it together, "thank you. Really, thank you."

Nic looks confused. "Uh . . . this isn't what I expected."

"Sorry, sorry." Harper wipes her eyes. "We've got a lot of explaining to do."

Harper and I sit down and tell Nic what happened. She nods intently all through the story.

"Why didn't you tell me?" Nic asks. "I like cats too! Not as much as dogs, but they're still cool."

"That's my fault," Harper says sheepishly. "I asked Avery not to tell you. I didn't want too many people to know."

Nic nods. "I get that. But wow, this is embarrassing. I really thought I was doing something here."

"You did," I assure her. "This is the first time I've laughed all week."

There's a short silence after that. We fidget a little, looking everywhere except at one another. Phantom's curled in my lap, almost asleep. I put a hand on her back for courage. I can do this.

"I'm sorry, Harper, for telling Dad and betraying you.

And I'm sorry for yelling at you, Nic. I was mean to you when you just wanted to help. I've been really terrible this week." I sniffle, trying not to burst into tears. "I don't know if you'll forgive me, but I really am sorry."

Harper and Nic look at each other, then back at me. Harper sighs, shaking her head. "No, I'm sorry, Avery. I shouldn't have screamed at you. That wasn't cool, and you and your dad were just trying to help."

"I'm sorry too," Nic blurts. "You're right, this is my fault. I shouldn't have made you sing in front of Mrs. Thompson. I feel terrible, honest."

I look at them both, a tiny bit of hope in my chest. "So . . . so you're not mad at me?"

"No!"

"Nope. Not even close."

I really do start crying now. And this time, it's with relief. A tiny bit of that weight is gone. They're still my friends.

"Aww, don't cry." Harper watches me anxiously while I wipe my eyes with my sleeve. "You're scaring the cat."

I laugh and hug Phantom tight. She squirms from my

arms and pads back into her closet to flop onto her bed. "Sorry, Phantom. But, Harper . . . are you okay?"

"Yeah. I mean it." Harper sits a little closer to me, not looking me in the eye. "I *was* mad at first. I wanted to live with Mom. But . . . I started staying with my aunt. She let me take a few days off from school to 'adjust,' as she called it."

"Do you like living with your aunt?" I ask, praying the answer is yes.

Harper nods. "She's really cool, even though her house is super messy. At first, I missed home, but I can't lie, it's nice to go to sleep with no screaming. So, I really should thank you, Avery. I know you were worried, and it worked out."

I want to start crying again. I'm overwhelmed—this, at least, I didn't ruin. "Can I hug you?"

Harper seems surprised but laughs. "Sure."

I hug Harper tight. She hugs me back, and I know she forgives me. When we break apart, Harper puts her hands on my shoulders. "Okay, now your turn. How can we help you? We're all worried about you."

I look at my shoes. I guess it's time to talk about it. "Dad is making me go to therapy. For my anxiety."

I hold my breath, waiting for them to tell me it's weird, but they just look at each other.

"Is that it?" Harper asks. "I thought you were already going."

"You don't think it's weird . . . ?"

"No! Everyone goes to therapy now," Nic says. "I went for a little while after Grandpa died. My whole family did."

What?! Nic's been to therapy before? The coolest girl in school? "What's it like? What do you do?"

"Someone just talked to us. And you answer questions and talk about how you're feeling." Nic shrugs. "It was fine. Not scary or anything."

I'm speechless. I can't believe this. I could have asked Nic about it the whole time. I'm an idiot.

"I think it'll really help you," Harper says to me. "You hold a lot of stuff in, you know. You can talk to someone now instead of throwing scripts at Thomas. Which was amazing, by the way."

Maybe they're right. Now I feel bad about yelling at Dad. He was just trying to help.

"Okay, what else?" Harper says after I'm quiet for a few seconds. "I'm in the mood to fix problems."

"This isn't a problem, but I just want to say something," Nic says. She looks at me and Harper intently. "I'm really glad we're all friends."

"We may be disasters, but we're way better than Amberleigh," Harper says, grinning.

I laugh, and Nic does too. "No, you're right. Amberleigh and I were friends because we had a lot of the same classes, but I guess I never felt like I was part of the group, you know? She never stayed at my house before. Not even once."

I remember Jamal's comment about me being Nic's "first friend." I guess this is what he meant. My chest warms at the thought. Nic was my first real friend, and I guess I was hers too.

"Anyway, that's all," Nic says, smiling at us. "Avery, what're you going to do with your cat? You can't take it home because of your brother."

"I'm not sure," I say, glancing at Phantom. "I guess we need to get a home for Phantom. If you found her, it's only a matter of time until everyone else does."

Harper nods thoughtfully. "True. Let me think about that. I have an idea, but I need to make sure it's okay." Harper looks at me, then Nic. Her expression turns a little mischievous. "Let's fix another problem. I think Nic has something to tell you."

I look at Nic in confusion, and Nic looks panicked.

"Harper," she hisses, but Harper edges toward the curtain.

"Wow, look at the time! Gotta go to class and leave you two alone!"

I wave at Harper uncertainly as she leaves, then look at Nic. Nic fidgets a little, not looking at me. "Umm . . . what did Harper mean?"

Nic looks into my eyes, and I'm suddenly really hot. Why is she looking at me like that?

"Actually, there's something I want to tell you."

"Umm, okay." My mouth is uncomfortably dry.

Nic fidgets again and wipes her palms on her jeans. "Umm, I don't know how to say it. Harper and me practiced, and I still don't know."

Oh God, what is it? My mind runs through a hundred possibilities at once. She's moving away. She's dying. Her mom is marrying my dad. Wait, that doesn't make sense, her mom is already married. Oh God, then that would be even worse!

"I like you, Avery. Like a lot."

"Umm." I don't know what she means. "I like you too? I mean, we're friends, right? We have to like each other a little, at least."

"No, I mean, like . . . really like you. In like a, uh, Romeo-Juliet kinda way. Juliet-Juliet in this case."

Oh.

For once in my life, my mind is completely blank.

"I should have told you earlier," Nic babbles, her face turning a delicate shade of red. "But I wasn't sure if you even liked girls, and when I tried to talk to you, you wouldn't say anything. So then I thought you hated me, but then I found out you just had anxiety, and I hoped maybe you'd like me too, but I still wasn't sure and oh God I'm talking so much." Nic's face is bright red now.

I stare at her for too long, trying to make sense of what she's telling me. Nic . . . likes me? Like I like her? She doesn't think I'm weird? Or disgusting, like Amberleigh said?

"Avery?" Nic asks, searching my face.

Anxiety rears up to choke me, as usual, but I stuff it back down. I can do this.

"I like you too."

Nic seems shocked. "Really?"

"Really!" I'm starting to feel excited instead of anxious. "I've liked you since I moved here! I thought you were straight!"

"Not even close!" Nic reaches for my hands, and I take hers. We grin at each other, and happiness swirls in my chest. I can't believe it. Wait, is this what Harper meant when she said I "might be surprised"? She was in on it the whole time. Oh my God.

"I can't believe it," Nic says, still grinning. "I never thought this would happen when I asked you to do the play."

Oh yeah. The play. I hold Nic's hand tighter. I need to be honest with her, like she was with me. "Nic, listen to me. I don't want to be Juliet. Like at all. I never have."

Nic surprises me by nodding. "I figured. It's been really hard on you, I know. I'm sorry again for pushing you."

"It's okay. But what will Mrs. Thompson say? Who can play Juliet?"

Nic shrugs. "Who cares? As long as you're okay, it doesn't matter."

Warmth spreads all over my body, but I try not to be too excited. It's not fair to her. She and Harper helped me practice so much. Harper worked hard to write it. We've gotta do *something*. But what? Who can play Juliet if not me? Who knows all the lines and can sing the part?

"And hey, silver lining! You won't have to kiss Thomas. He's gross."

We both laugh. She's so close to me. I can smell the honey scent of her shampoo. I feel like I can do anything at the moment. Everything's working out. I just have to be brave one more time.

"But there is someone I would like to kiss."

Nic's eyes get really big, and then they soften. She moves closer to me, so close I can feel her breath on my face. "Me too."

I'm so nervous. I'm really sweaty, like always. But I take a deep breath and close my eyes and press my lips to hers.

It's short and sweet and perfect. For just a moment, I forget about the play, and therapy, and our fights. For a second, I'm really, truly happy.

We break apart, still holding hands, still smiling. She's so beautiful, and smart, and positive, and she helped me so much with the play even though she didn't have to . . . Wait. Wait! That's it!

I squeeze her hands in mine, grinning. "I think I know what to do about the play."

Chapter 34

"Can I tell you a secret?" Thomas asks. His face is pale under the harsh stage lights, and for once, he looks nervous. At least the makeup covered up the bruise on his temple. He glances at me, and I give him a thumbs-up.

"Of course," Nic says, her voice shaking a little. It's almost time.

"I don't even like donuts," Thomas says. The cue for the first song.

Nic opens her mouth, and I do too. This is the first song we all sing together. She sings, but she's not singing the Juliet part. I am.

I'm backstage, with a microphone. Nic is playing Juliet—she knew all my parts anyway, so it was perfect. Emily stepped up to play Nic's part, and the play was saved. And I can sing without anyone watching. I close my eyes, and the melody fills my ears, my bones. This is the first time I've actually enjoyed singing the songs.

I stay in the back, singing when it's time, helping the crew when Nic and Thomas are just talking. And I'm not anxious. Not even a little. The crew is where I belong, where I always have. I'm glad I tried to play the part because it helped me be friends with Nic and Harper, but I'm even more glad Mrs. Thompson let me stay in the back. I feel better than I have in days. I even ate dinner last night.

It's not long before the play's over. The actors take the stage as the audience cheers. I clap as hard as I can.

"Nic Pearson as Juliet!" Mrs. Thompson calls. Nic bows and the audience screams. "And Avery Williams as Juliet's vocals!"

My face heats up as the crew pushes me onstage. Nic holds out her hand to me, and when I take it, I don't feel so bad. We bow together, and everyone yells and cheers. While Mrs. Thompson calls out the other names, Nic and

I look at each other, holding hands, and I don't know if I'll ever feel this happy again.

After Mrs. Thompson is done, she comes to me and Nic. She's smiling. "Great job tonight, girls. I knew you both could do it."

"Thanks, Mrs. Thompson."

"Hey!" Harper waves at us from backstage. "Look who's here!"

I look behind her, and tears well up in my eyes. It's Dad. He came.

I run to him, and he engulfs me in a huge hug. "Oh, I see we're on speaking terms again, huh?"

"I can't believe you came." I hug him tight. "I'm sorry I yelled at you, Dad. I don't hate you."

"I know." Dad lets me go and puts one hand on my shoulder. Maybe I'm seeing things, but his eyes seem a little watery too. "You sounded amazing. I'm so proud of you, Avery."

"You two make me sick," Andrew says from behind, but he's smiling.

Nic joins her family, and it's one big party. I meet Harper's aunt, who's bubbly and always laughing, and Nic's whole crew is here. I'm beaming the entire time. Harper says we should go to Waffle House after we clean the theater, and everyone agrees.

"One second," I say, and run to the back of the theater. I open Phantom's closet one more time. Harper really was in a fixing mood, because she convinced her aunt to take Phantom in. I'm so glad she'll have a real house to live in and real food every day instead of just turkey sandwiches. I'll miss her, but Harper said I can visit her any time I want. I have a feeling Nic, Harper, and I have a lot more sleepovers in our future.

Phantom looks up at me from her cat bed, then gets to her feet, purring. I cradle her in my arms.

"I did it, Phantom. I did the play. Not the way I thought, but I did it." She purrs and nuzzles her head against my cheek. I hold her for a long time as the noise in the theater dies down. I'm calm and happy, and Phantom, Nic, and Harper all helped me get here. I hug her to my chest, then put her down in the cat carrier Harper gave me. "Thanks for being my cat therapist for so long, Phantom. I promise I'll let you know how real therapy goes. Now, come on. You've gotta meet your new family, and I'm going to hang out with my friends. And my *girlfriend*." That's gonna take getting used to. I pet her ears and zip up her carrier. She flops onto her side and yawns, still purring. "Let's go."

I close the closet door behind us and join everyone waiting for me.

Acknowledgments

Innumerable thanks, as always, to Grandma. You are kind and wonderful, and I'm so blessed to have you as a grandmother. You're also the best plotting buddy, despite being completely uninterested in both cats and theater.

Big thank you to my wonderful agent, Holly Root! Thank you for your patience, and for sending me the "do you like cats?" email that started it all. Huge thanks also to my amazing editor, Olivia Valcarce, the pun-master and best editor a girl could ask for.

Emily Chapman, you are my best friend and a rockstar. I'm so glad you're in my life (and I am very grateful for your iconic live tweets whenever you read my books).

Tas, my beloved CP and friend—you are one of my favorite people on this planet. Thank you so much for reading the worst first draft I've ever written and staying up late to listen to my absolute nonsense.

J. Elle! Thank you for reading the first three chapters and telling me this story has legs. And for sending me pictures of the cutest dog in the world, Max! And thank you, SJ, for cheering me on every day while I was drafting this story.

Thank you to my writing groups: the slackers, WiM, Scream Town, AltChat, AoCs. I love you all dearly. Thank you for the laughs, the tears, the overwhelming love and support. I owe y'all so much.

And finally, thank you, younger me, for staying. We made it.

Find more reads you will love . . .

Kat loves walking her neighbor's irresistible pug, Meatball. So Kat turns her hobby into something she can do with all her friends: Four Paws Dog Walking is in business! But wrangling puppies and pleasing customers turns out to be harder than they thought. Can Kat keep taking care of the dogs she loves without hurting her friendships?

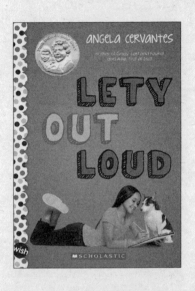

Since Lety's first language is Spanish, she loves volunteering at the Furry Friends Animal Shelter, where the pets don't care if she can't find the right word. When the shelter needs someone to write animal profiles, Lety jumps at the chance. Grumpy classmate Hunter also wants to write profiles, so he devises a secret competition between them. But if the shelter finds out about the contest, will Lety be allowed to adopt her favorite dog?

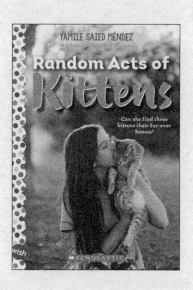

When Natalia finds a lost cat with a litter of newborn kittens, she's desperate to keep one of them. Whether or not her mami says yes to a new pet, the rest of the kitties will need homes—so Natalia starts an anonymous online account to find each cat the purrfect owner. But as her classmates apply, her matchmaking scheme gets more complicated. And what will Natalia do when her *former* best friend applies for a kitten?

Best friends Nadine and Daniel always make time to catch up over pumpkin spice lattes. But their routine is shaken up when a new girl, Kiya, starts at their school. Daniel falls for Kiya the second he sees her. Which would be fine . . . if Nadine hadn't recently realized she might be falling for Daniel herself. Nadine knows she has to find the courage to tell Daniel how she feels, but what if she's already lost her shot?

Homeschooled Amelia can't wait to start regular school for the first time . . . but the transition is much harder than she imagined. Everything about her seems wrong, from her clothes to her hobbies. So when Amelia starts to volunteer at an alpaca ranch, she's overjoyed to be doing something she's good at—taking care of animals. But when the alpacas are put in mortal peril, can Amelia save the only place that's ever felt like home?

Have you read all the (wish) books?

- ☐ *Clementine for Christmas* by Daphne Benedis-Grab
- ☐ *Carols and Crushes* by Natalie Blitt
- ☐ *Snow One Like You* by Natalie Blitt
- ☐ *Allie, First at Last* by Angela Cervantes
- ☐ *Gaby, Lost and Found* by Angela Cervantes
- ☐ *Lety Out Loud* by Angela Cervantes
- ☐ *Alpaca My Bags* by Jenny Goebel
- ☐ *Sit, Stay, Love* by J. J. Howard
- ☐ *Pugs and Kisses* by J. J. Howard
- ☐ *Pugs in a Blanket* by J. J. Howard
- ☐ *The Love Pug* by J. J. Howard
- ☐ *Girls Just Wanna Have Pugs* by J. J. Howard
- ☐ *The Boy Project* by Kami Kinard
- ☐ *Best Friend Next Door* by Carolyn Mackler
- ☐ *11 Birthdays* by Wendy Mass
- ☐ *Finally* by Wendy Mass
- ☐ *13 Gifts* by Wendy Mass
- ☐ *The Last Present* by Wendy Mass
- ☐ *Graceful* by Wendy Mass
- ☐ *Twice Upon a Time: Beauty and the Beast, the Only One Who Didn't Run Away* by Wendy Mass
- ☐ *Twice Upon a Time: Rapunzel, the One with All the Hair* by Wendy Mass

THE SECRET DOOR
TO SUCCESS

By

FLORENCE SCOVEL SHINN

DeVorss Publications
Camarillo, California

CONTENTS

———————

The Secret Door to Success
Copyright © 1940 by Florence Scovel Shinn
ISBN: 087516-257-6

DeVorss & Company, PO Box 1389, Camarillo CA 93011-1389
w w w . d e v o r s s . c o m

Printed in the United States of America

THE SECRET DOOR TO SUCCESS

"So the people shouted when the priests blew with the trumpets: and it came to pass, when the people heard the sound of the trumpet, and the people shouted with a great shout, that the wall fell down flat, so that the people went up into the city, every man straight before him, and they took the city." — Joshua 6:20.

A successful man is always asked — "What is the secret of your success?"

People never ask a man who is a failure, "What is the secret of your failure?" It is quite easy to see and they are not interested.

People all want to know how to open the secret door of success.

For each man there is success, but it seems to be behind a door or wall. In the Bible reading, we have heard the wonderful story of the falling of the walls of Jericho.

Of course all biblical stories have a metaphysical interpretation.

We will talk now about *your* wall of Jericho: the wall separating *you* from success. Nearly everyone has built a wall around his own Jericho.

This city you are not able to enter, contains great treasures; your divinely designed success, your heart's desire!

7

What kind of wall have you built around your Jericho? Often, it is a wall of resentment—resenting someone, or resenting a situation, shuts off your good.

If you are a failure and resent the success of someone else, you are keeping away your own success.

I have given the following statement to neutralize envy and resentment.

What God has done for others, He now does for me and more.

A woman was filled with envy because a friend had received a gift, she made this statement, and an exact duplicate of the gift was given her—plus another present.

It was when the children of Israel shouted, that the walls of Jericho fell down. When you make an affirmation of Truth, your wall of Jericho totters.

I gave the following statement to a woman: *The walls of lack and delay now crumble away, and I enter my Promised Land, under grace.* She had a vivid picture of stepping over a fallen wall, and received the demonstration of her good, almost immediately.

It is the word of realization which brings about a change in your affairs; for words and thoughts are a form of radio-activity.

Taking an interest in your work, enjoying what you are doing opens the secret door to success.

A number of years ago I went to California to speak at the different centers, by way of the Panama Canal, and on the boat I met a man named Jim Tully.

For years he had been a tramp. He called himself The King of the Hoboes.

He was ambitious and picked up an education.

He had a vivid imagination and commenced writing stories about his experiences.

He dramatized tramp life, he enjoyed what he was doing, and became a very successful author. I remember one book called "Outside Looking In." It was made into a motion picture.

He is now famous and prosperous and lives in Hollywood. What opened the secret door to success for Jim Tully?

Dramatizing his life — being interested in what he was doing, he made the most of being a tramp. On the boat, we all sat at the captain's table, which gave us a chance to talk.

Mrs. Grace Stone was also a passenger on the boat; she had written the "Bitter Tea of General Yen," and was going to Hollywood to have it made into a moving-picture: she had lived in China and was inspired to write the book.

That is the *Secret* of Success, to *make what you are doing interesting to other people.* Be interested yourself, and others will find you interesting.

A good disposition, a smile, often opens the secret door; the Chinese say, "A man without a smiling face, must not open a shop."

The success of a smile was brought out in a French moving-picture in which Chevalier took the lead, the picture was called, "With a Smile." One of the characters had become poor, dreary and almost a derelict; He said to Chevalier "What good has my honesty done me?" Chevalier replied,

"Even honesty won't help you, without a smile:" so the man changes on the spot, cheers up, and becomes very successful.

Living in the past, complaining of your misfortunes, builds a thick wall around your Jericho.

Talking too much about your affairs, scattering your forces, brings you up against a high wall. I knew a man of brains and ability, who was a complete failure.

He lived with his mother and aunt, and I found that every night when he went home to dinner, he told them all that had taken place during the day at the office; he discussed his hopes, his fears, and his failures.

I said to him, "You scatter your forces by talking about your affairs. Don't discuss your business with your family. Silence is Golden!"

He took my lead. During dinner he refused to talk about business, His mother and aunt were in despair: They loved to hear all about everything; but his silence proved golden!

Not long after, he was given a position at one hundred dollars a week, and in a few years, he had a salary of three hundred dollars a week.

Success is not a secret, it is a System.

Many people are up against the wall of discouragement. Courage and endurance are part of the system. We read this in lives of all successful men and women.

I had an amusing experience which brought this to my notice. I went to a moving picture theatre to meet a friend.

While waiting, I stood near a young boy, selling programs.

He called to people passing, "Buy a complete program of the picture, containing photographs of the actors and a sketch of their lives."

Most people passed by without buying. To my great surprise, he suddenly turned to me, and said —"Say, this ain't no racket for a guy with ambition!"

Then he gave a discourse on success. He said, "Most people give up just before something big is coming to them. A successful man never gives up."

Of course I was interested and said, "I'll bring you a book the next time I come. It is called *The Game of Life and How to Play It*. You will agree with a lot of the ideas."

A week or two later I went back with the book.

The girl at the ticket office said to him —"Let me read it, Eddie, while you are selling programs." The man who took tickets leaned over to see what it was about.

"The Game of Life" always gets people's interest.

I returned to the theatre in about three weeks, Eddie had gone. He had expanded into a new job that he liked. His wall of Jericho had crumbled, he had refused to be discouraged.

Only twice, is the word *success* mentioned in the Bible—both times in the Book of Joshua.

"Only be strong and very courageous to observe to do according to all the law which Moses, my servant, commanded thee: turn not from it to the right nor to the left, that thou mayest have good success whithersoever thou goest. This book of the law shall not depart from thy mouth, but thou

shalt meditate therein day and night, that thou mayest observe to do all that is written therein, for then shalt thou make thy way prosperous and thou shalt have good success. Turn not to the right nor to the left."

The *road to success* is a *straight and narrow path; it is a road of loving absorption, of undivided attention.*

"You attract the things you give a great deal of thought to."

So if you give a great deal of thought to lack, you attract lack, if you give a great deal of thought to injustice, you attract more injustice.

Joshua said, "And it shall come to pass, that when they make a long blast with the ram's horn, and when ye hear the sound of the trumpet, all the people shall shout with a great shout: and the wall of the city shall fall down flat, and the people shall ascend up, every man straight before him."

The inner meaning of this story, is the power of the word, your word which dissolves obstacles, and removes barriers.

When the people shouted the walls fell down.

We find in folk-lore and fairy stories, which come down from legends founded on Truth, the same idea — a word opens a door or cleaves a rock.

We have it again in the Arabian Night's Story, "Ali Baba and The Forty Thieves." I saw it made into a moving picture.

Ali Baba has a secret hiding place, hidden somewhere behind rocks and mountains, the entrance may only be gained by speaking a secret word. — It is "Open Sesame!"

Ali Baba faces the mountain and cries — "Open Sesame!" and the rocks slide apart.

It is very inspiring, for it gives you the realization of how YOUR own rocks and barriers, *will part at the right word.*

So let us now take the statement — The walls of lack and delay now crumble away, and I enter my Promised Land, under grace.

BRICKS WITHOUT STRAW

"There shall no straw be given you, yet ye shall make bricks without straw." — Exodus 5:18.

In the 5th chapter of Exodus, we have a picture of every day life, when giving a metaphysical interpretation.

The Children of Israel were in bondage to Pharaoh, the cruel taskmaster, ruler of Egypt. They were kept in slavery, making bricks, and were hated and despised.

Moses had orders from the Lord to deliver his people from bondage — "Moses and Aaron went in and told Pharaoh — Thus saith the Lord God of Israel, Let my people go, that they may hold a feast unto me in the wilderness."

He not only refused to let them go, but told them he would make their tasks even more difficult: they must make bricks without straw being provided for them.

"And the task-masters of the people went out, and their officers, and they spake to the people, saying, Thus saith Pharaoh, I will not give you straw."

14

"Go ye, get you straw where ye can find it: yet not ought of your work shall be diminished."

It was impossible to make bricks without straw. The Children of Israel were completely crushed by Pharaoh, they were beaten for not producing the bricks—Then came the message from Jehovah.

"Go therefore now, and work; for there shall no straw be given you, yet shall ye deliver the tale (number) of bricks."

Working with Spiritual law they could make bricks without straw, which means to accomplish the seemingly impossible.

How often in life people are confronted with this situation.

Agnes M. Lawson in her "Hints to Bible Students" says—"The Life in Egypt under foreign oppression is the symbol of man under the hard taskmasters of Destructive thinking, Pride, Fear, Resentment, Ill-will, etc. The deliverance under Moses is the freedom man gains from the taskmasters, as he learns the law of life, for we can never come under grace, except we first know the law. The law must be made known in order to be fulfilled."

In the 111th Psalm we read in the final verse, "The fear of the Lord (law) is the beginning of Wisdom: a good understanding have all they that do his commandments: his praise endureth forever."

Now if we read the word Lord (law) it will give us the key to the statement.

The fear of the law (Karmic law) is the beginning of wisdom (not the fear of the Lord).

When we know that whatever we send out comes back, we begin to be afraid of our own boomerangs.

I read in a medical journal the following facts telling of the Boomerang this great Pharaoh received.

"It would appear that flesh is indeed heir to a long and ancient line of ills, when, as was revealed by Lord Monyahan at a lecture at Leeds, that the Pharaoh of the oppression suffered from hardening of the heart in a literal sense; Lord Monyahan showed some remarkable photographic slides of results of surgical operations a thousand years before Christ, and among these was a slide of the actual anatomical remains of the Pharaoh of the Oppression.

"The large vessel springing from the heart was in such a well-preserved state, as to enable sections of it to be made and compared with those made recently from the lantern slide. It was impossible to distinguish between the ancient and modern vessel. Both hearts had been attacked by Atheroma, a condition in which calcium salts are deposited in the walls of the vessel, making it rigid and inelastic.

"Inadequate expanse to the stream of blood from the heart caused the vessel to give way; with this condition went the mental changes that occur with a rigid arterial system: *A narrowness of outlook; restriction and dread of enterprise, a literal hardening of the heart.*"

So Pharaoh's hardness of heart, hardened his own heart.

This is as true today as it was several thousand years ago—we are all coming out of the Land of Egypt, out of the House of Bondage.

Your doubts and fears keep you in slavery; you face a situation which seems hopeless; What can you do? It is a case of making bricks without straw.

But remember the words of Jehovah, "Go therefore now, and work; for there shall no straw be given you, yet shall ye deliver the tale (number) of bricks."

You shall make bricks without straw. God makes a way where there is no way!

I was told the story of a woman who needed money for her rent: it was necessary to have it at once, she knew of no channel, she had exhausted every avenue.

However, she was a Truth student, and kept making her affirmations. Her dog whined and wanted to go out, she put on his leash and walked down the street, in the accustomed direction.

However, the dog pulled at his leash and wanted to go in another direction.

She followed, and in the middle of the block, opposite an open park, she looked down, and picked up a roll of bills, which exactly covered her rent.

She looked for ads, but never found the owner. There were no houses near where she found it.

The reasoning mind, the intellect, takes the throne of Pharaoh in your consciousness. It says continually, "It can't be done. What's the use!"

We must drown out these dreary suggestions with a vital affirmation!

For example take this statement: *"The unexpected happens, my seemingly impossible good now comes to pass."* This stops all argument from the army of the aliens (the reasoning mind).

"The unexpected happens!" That is an idea it cannot cope with.

"Thou hast made me wiser than mine enemies." Your enemy thoughts, your doubts, fears and apprehensions!

Think of the joy of really being free forever, from the Pharaoh of the oppression. To have the idea of security, health, happiness and abundance established in the subconscious. It would mean a life free from all limitation!

It would be the Kingdom which Jesus Christ spoke of, where all things are automatically added unto us. I say automatically added unto us, because all life is vibration; and when we vibrate to success, happiness and abundance, the things which symbolize these states of consciousness will attach themselves to us.

Feel rich and successful, and suddenly you receive a large cheque or a beautiful gift.

I tell the story showing the working of this law. I went to a party where people played games, and whoever won, received a gift. The prize was a beautiful fan.

Among those present, was a very rich woman, who had everything. Her name was Clara. The poorer and resentful ones got together and whispered: "We hope Clara doesn't get the fan." Of course Clara won the fan.

She was care-free and vibrating to abundance. *Envy and resentment short-circuit your good* and keep away your fans.

If you should happen to be resentful and envious, take the statement; *What God has done for others He now does for me and more!*

Then all the fans and things will come your way.

No man gives to himself but himself, and no man takes away from himself but himself: the "Game of Life" is a game of solitaire; as you change, all conditions will change.

Now to go back to Pharaoh the oppressor; no one loves an oppressor.

I remember a friend I had many years ago, her name was Lettie; her father had plenty of money and supplied her mother and herself with food and clothes, but no luxuries.

We went to Art School together, and all the students would buy reproductions of the "Winged Victory," "Whistler's Mother" or something to bring art into their homes.

My friend's father called all these things "plunder." He would say, "Don't bring home any plunder."

So she lived a colorless life without a "Winged Victory" on her bureau or "Whistler's Mother" on the wall.

He would say often to my friend and her mother, "When I die, you'll both be well off."

One day someone said to Lettie, "When are you going abroad?" (all art students went abroad.)

She replied, cheerfully, "Not 'till Papa dies."

So people always look forward to being free from lack and oppression.

Let us now free ourselves from the *tyrants of negative thinking:* we have been slaves to doubts, fears and apprehension and let us be delivered as Moses delivered the Children of Israel; and come out of the Land of Egypt, out of the House of Bondage.

Find the thought which is your great oppressor; find the *King-Pin.*

In the logging camps in the Spring, the logs are sent down the rivers in great numbers.

Sometimes the logs become crossed and cause a jam; the men look for the log causing the jam (they call it the King-Pin), straighten it, and the logs rush down the river again.

Maybe your King-Pin is resentment, resentment holds back your good.

The more you resent, the more you will have to resent; you grow a resentment track in your brain, and your expression will be one of habitual resentment.

You will be avoided and miss the golden opportunities which await you each day.

I remember a few years ago, the streets were filled with men selling apples.

They got up early to get the good corners.

I passed one several times on Park Avenue, he had the most disagreeable expression I have ever seen.

As people passed he said, "Apples! Apples!" but no one stopped to buy.

I invested in an apple and said, "You'll never sell apples unless you change your expression."

He replied, "Well that guy over there took my corner."

I said, "Never mind about the corner, you can sell apples right here if you'll look pleasant."

He said "O.K. lady," and I went on. The next day I saw him, his whole expression had changed; he was doing a big business, selling apples with a smile.

So find your King-Pin—(you may have more than one); and your logs of *success, happiness and abundance will go rushing down your river.*

"Go therefore now and work, for there shall no straw be given you, yet ye shall make bricks without straw."

"AND FIVE OF THEM WERE WISE"

"And five of them were wise, and five were foolish. They that were foolish took their lamps, and took no oil with them" — Math. 25:2:3.

My subject is the parable of the Wise and the Foolish Virgins. "And five of them were wise, and five were foolish. They that were foolish took their lamps, and took no oil with them. But the wise took oil in their vessels with their lamps." The parable teaches that true prayer means preparation.

Jesus Christ said, "And all things, whatsoever ye shall ask in prayer, *believing*, ye shall receive" (Math. 21:22). "Therefore I say unto you, what things soever ye desire, when ye pray, believe that ye receive them, and ye shall have them" (Mark 11:24). In this parable he shows that only those who have prepared for their good (thereby showing active faith) will bring the manifestation to pass.

We might paraphrase the scriptures and say: When ye pray believe ye have it. When ye pray ACT as if you have already received.

Armchair faith or rocking chair faith, will never move mountains. In the armchair, in the silence,

or meditation, you are filled with the wonder of this Truth, and feel that your faith will never waver. You know that The Lord is your Shepherd, you shall never want.

You feel that your God of Plenty will wipe out all burdens of debt or limitations. Then you leave your armchair and step out into the arena of Life. It is only what you do in the arena that counts.

I will give you an illustration showing how the law works; for faith without action is dead.

A man, one of my students, had a great desire to go abroad. He took the statement: *I give thanks for my divinely designed trip, divinely financed, under grace, in a perfect way.* He had very little money, but knowing the law of preparation, he bought a trunk. It was a very gay and happy trunk with a big red band around its waist. Whenever he looked at it it gave him a realization of a trip. One day he seemed to feel his room moving. He felt the motion of a ship. He went to the window to breathe the fresh air, and it smelt like the aroma of the docks. With his inner ear he heard the shriek of a sea-gull and the creaking of the gang-plank. The trunk had commenced to work. It had put him in the vibration of his trip. Soon after that, a large sum of money came to him and he took the trip. He said afterwards that it was perfect in every detail.

In the arena of Life we must keep ourselves tuned-up to concert pitch.

Are we acting from motives of fear or faith? *Watch your motives with all diligence, for out of them are the issues of life.*

If your problem is a financial one (and it usually

is), you must know how to wind yourself up financially, and keep wound up by always acting your faith. The material attitude towards money is to trust in your salary, your income and investments, which can shrink over night.

The spiritual attitude toward money is to trust in God for your supply. To keep your possessions, always realize that they are God in manifestation. "What Allah has given cannot be diminished," then if one door shuts another door, immediately, opens.

Never voice lack or limitation for "by your words you are condemned." You combine with what you notice, and if you are always noticing failure and hard times, you will combine with failure and hard times.

You must form the habit of living in the fourth dimension, "The World of the Wondrous." It is the world where you do not judge by appearances.

You have trained your inner eye to see through failure into success, to see through sickness into health to see through limitation into plenty. I will give you the land which your inner eye sees. "I will give to you the land which thou seeth."

The man who achieves success has the *fixed idea of success.* If it is founded on a rock of truth and rightness it will stand. If not, it is built upon sand and washed into the sea, returning to its native nothingness.

Only divine ideas can endure. Evil destroys itself, for it is a cross current against universal order, and the way of the transgressor is hard.

"They that were foolish took their lamps, and

took no oil with them. But the wise took oil in their vessels with their lamps."

The lamp symbolizes man's consciousness. The oil is what brings Light or understanding.

"While the bridegroom tarried, they all slumbered and slept. And at midnight there was a cry made, Behold, the bridegroom cometh; go ye out to meet him. Then all those virgins arose, and trimmed their lamps. And the foolish said unto the wise, Give us your oil; for our lamps are gone out."

The foolish virgins were without wisdom or understanding, which is oil for the consciousness, and when they were confronted with a serious situation, they had no way of handling it.

And when they said to the wise "give us of your oil," the wise answered saying, "Not so; lest there be not enough for us and you: but go ye rather to them that sell, and buy for yourselves."

That means that the foolish virgins could *not receive more than was in their consciousness,* or what they were vibrating to.

The man received the trip because it was in his consciousness, as a reality. He believed that he had already received. As he prepared for the trip he was taking oil for his lamps. With *realization comes manifestation.*

The law of preparation works both ways. If you prepare for what you fear or don't want, you begin to attract it. David said, "The thing I feared has come upon me." We hear people say, "I must put away money in case of illness." They are deliberately preparing to be ill. Or, "I'm saving for a

rainy day." The rainy day is sure to come, at a most inconvenient time.

The divine idea for every man is plenty. Your barns *should be* full, and your cup *should* flow over, but we must learn to ask aright.

For example take this statement: *I call on the law of accumulation. My supply comes from God, and now pours in and piles up, under grace.*

This statement does not give any picture of stint or saving or sickness. It gives a fourth dimensional feeling of abundance, leaving the channels to Infinite Intelligence.

Every day you must make a choice, will you be wise or foolish? Will you prepare for your good? Will you *take the giant swing into faith?* Or serve doubt and fear and bring no oil for your lamps?

"And while they went to buy, the bridegroom came; and they that were ready went in with him to the marriage: and the door was shut. Afterward came also the other virgins, saying, Lord, Lord, open to us. But he answered and said, Verily I say unto you, I know you not."

You may feel that the foolish virgins paid very dearly for neglecting to bring oil for their lamps, but we are dealing with the law of Karma (or the law of come back). It has been called the "judgement day," which people usually associate with the end of the world.

Your judgement day comes, they say, in sevens—seven hours, seven days, seven weeks, seven months, or seven years. It might even come in seven minutes. Then you pay some Karmic debt; the price for having violated spiritual law.

You failed to trust God, you took no oil for your lamps.

Every day examine your consciousness and see just what you are preparing for. You are fearful of lack and hang on to every cent, thereby attracting more lack. Use what you have with wisdom and it opens the way for more to come to you.

In my book, "Your Word Is Your Wand," I tell about the Magic Purse. In the Arabian Nights they tell the story of a man who had a Magic Purse. As money went out, immediately money appeared in it again.

So I made the statement: *My supply comes from God—I have the magic purse of the spirit. It can never be depleted. As money goes out, immediately money comes in. It is always crammed, jammed with abundance, under grace, in perfect ways.*

This brings a vivid picture to mind: You are drawing on the bank of the imagination.

A woman who did not have much money was afraid to pay any bills and see her bank account dwindle. It came to her with great conviction: "I have the magic purse of the spirit. It can never be depleted. As money goes out, immediately, money comes in." She fearlessly paid her bills, and several large cheques came to her that she did not expect.

"Watch and pray lest ye enter into the temptation" of preparing for something destructive instead of something constructive.

I knew a woman who told me she always kept a long crepe veil handy in case of funerals. I said to her, "You are a menace to your relatives, and are

preparing to hurry them all off, so that you can wear the veil." She destroyed it.

Another woman who had no money decided to send her two daughters to college. Her husband scorned the idea and said, "Who will pay their tuition? I have no money for it." She replied, "I know some *unforeseen good will come to us.*" She kept on preparing her daughters for college. Her husband laughed heartily and told all their friends that his wife was sending the girls to college on "some unforeseen good." A rich relative suddenly sent her a large sum of money. "Some unforeseen good" *did* arrive, for she had shown active faith. I asked what she had said to her husband when the cheque arrived. She replied, "Oh, I never antagonize George by telling him I am in the right."

So prepare for your "unforeseen good." Let every thought and every act express your unwavering faith. Every event in your life is a crystallized idea. Something you have invited through either fear or faith. *Something you have prepared for.*

So let us be wise and bring oil for our lamps— and when we least expect it, we shall reap the fruits of our faith.

My lamps are now filled with the oil of faith and fulfillment.

WHAT DO YOU EXPECT?

According to your faith be it unto you. — Matt.9:29

Faith is expectancy, "According to your faith, be it unto you."

We might say, according to your expectancies be it done unto you; so, what are you expecting?

We hear people say: "We expect the worst to happen," or "The worst is yet to come." They are deliberately inviting the worst to come.

We hear others say: "I expect a change for the better." They are inviting better conditions into their lives.

Change your expectancies and you change your conditions.

How can you change your expectancies, when you have formed the habit of expecting loss, lack or failure?

Begin to act as if you *expected* success, happiness and abundance; *prepare for your good.*

Do something to show you expect it to come. Active faith alone, will impress the subconscious.

If you have spoken the word for a home, prepare for it immediately, as if you hadn't a moment to lose. Collect little ornaments, table-cloths, etc. etc.!

I knew a woman who made the giant swing into faith, by buying a large arm-chair; a chair meant business, she bought a large and comfortable chair, for she was preparing for the right man. He came.

Someone will say, "Suppose you haven't money to buy ornaments or a chair?" Then look in shop windows and link with them in thought.

Get in their vibration: I sometimes hear people say; "I don't go into the shops because I can't afford to buy anything." That is just the reason you should go into the shops. Begin to make friends with the things you desire or require.

I know a woman who wanted a ring. She went boldly to the ring department and tried on rings.

It gave her such a realization of ownership, that not long after, a friend made her a gift of a ring. "You combine with what you notice."

Keep on noticing beautiful things, and you make an invisible contact. Sooner or later these things are drawn into your life, unless you say, "Poor me, too good to be true."

"My soul, wait thou only upon God: for my expectation is from Him." This is a most important statement from the 62nd Psalm.

The soul is the subconscious mind, and the psalmist was telling his subconscious to expect everything directly from the universal; not to depend upon doors and channels; "My expectation is from Him."

God cannot fail, for "His ways are ingenious, His methods are sure."

You can expect any seemingly impossible Good from God; if you do not limit the channels.

Do not say how you want it done, or how it can't be done.

"God is the Giver and the Gift *and creates His own amazing channels.*"

Take the following statement: *I cannot be separated from God the Giver, therefore, I cannot be separated from God the Gift. The gift is God in action.*

Get the realization that every blessing is *Good in action,* and see God in every face and good in every situation: This makes you master of all conditions.

A woman came to me saying that there was no heat in the radiators in their apartment, and that her mother was suffering from the cold. She added, "The landlord has declared that we can't have heat until a certain date:" I replied, "God is your landlord." She said, "That's all I want to know," and rushed out. That evening the heat was turned on without asking. It was because she realized that the landlord was God in manifestation.

This is a wonderful age, for people are becoming Miracle Minded; it is in the air.

Quoting from an article which I found in the New York Journal and American by John Anderson, it corroborates what I have just said.

The title of the article is "Theatre Goers Make Hits of Metaphysical Plays."

If, said a cynical manager, who shall be called Brock Pemberton, with a slight accent of sarcasm in his voice, the other night, on an intermission curbside talk, you fellows, meaning the critics, know so much about what the New York public

wants, why don't you tell me what to produce? Why don't you run me into business instead of out of it? "Why don't you tell me what sort of play the play-goers want to see?" "I would," I said, "But you wouldn't believe it."

"You're hedging," he said, "You don't know, and you're trying to cover up by pretending to know more than you're willing to say. You haven't any more idea than I have this minute what sort of plays generally succeed."

"I have," I said, "there is one sure fire success; one theme that works and has always worked, whether it is competing with boy meets girl, mysteries, historical tragedies, etc.; no play on the theme has ever completely failed if it had any merit at all, and a lot of poor ones have been big hits."

"You're stalling again," said Mr. Pemberton, "What sort of plays are they?"

"Metaphysical," I said, fouling slightly with a big word and waiting quietly for the effect. "Metaphysical," said Mr. Pemberton, "You mean metaphysical?"

I paused a moment and since Mr. Pemberton said nothing, went right on spouting such titles as "The Green Pastures," "The Star Wagon," "Father Malachy's Miracle!, etc." "Some of these," I added, "reached the public *over* the heads of the critics." But Mr. Pemberton had departed to ask probably, in every theatre in town, "Is there a metaphysician in the house?"

People are beginning to realize the power of

their words and thoughts. They understand *why* "Faith *is* the substance of the thing hoped for, the evidence of things not seen."

We see the law of expectancy working out through superstition.

If you walk under a ladder and expect it to give you bad luck, it will give you bad luck. The ladder is quite innocent; bad luck came because you expected it.

We might say, expectancy is the substance of the things hoped for; or expectancy is the substance of the thing man fears; "The thing I expected has come upon me."

Nothing is too good to be true, nothing is too wonderful to happen, nothing is too good to last; when you look to God for your good.

Now think of the blessings which seem so far off, and begin to expect them *now,* under grace, in an unexpected way; for God works in unexpected ways, His wonders to perform.

I was told that there are three thousand promises in the Bible.

Let us now expect all these blessings to come to pass. Among them we are promised Riches and Honor, Eternal Youth ("Your flesh shall become as a little child's) and Eternal Life, "death itself shall be overcome."

Christianity is founded upon the forgiveness of sins and an empty tomb.

We now know that all these things are scientifically possible.

As we call on the law of forgiveness, we become

free from mistakes and the consequences of mistakes. ("Though your sins be as scarlet ye shall be washed whiter than wool.")

Then our bodies will be bathed in Light, and express the "body electric," which is incorruptible and indestructible, pure substance, expressing perfection.

I expect the unexpected, my glorious good now comes to pass.

THE LONG ARM OF GOD

"The Eternal God is thy refuge, and underneath are the everlasting arms." — Deut. 33:27

In the bible, the arm of God always symbolizes protection. The writers of the bible knew the power of a symbol. It brings a picture which impresses the subconscious mind. They used the symbols of the rock, sheep, shepherds, vineyard, lamp, and hundreds of others. It would be interesting to know how many symbols are used in the bible. The arm also symbolizes strength.

"The eternal God is thy refuge, and underneath are the everlasting arms: and he shall thrust out the enemy from before thee; and shall say, Destroy them."

Who is the enemy "before thee." The negative thought-forms which you have built up in your subconscious mind. A man's enemies are only those of his own household. The everlasting arms thrust out these enemy thoughts and destroy them.

Have you ever felt the relief of getting out some negative thought-form? Perhaps you have built up a thought-form of resentment, until you are always boiling with anger about something. You

resent people you know, people you don't know—people in the past and people in the present; and you may be sure that the people in the future won't escape your wrath.

All the organs of the body are affected by resentment—for when you resent, you resent with every organ of the body. You pay the penalty with rheumatism, arthritis, neuritis, etc., for acid thoughts produce acid in the blood. All this trouble comes because you are fighting the battle, not leaving it to the long arm of God.

I have given the following statement to many of my students. *The long arm of God reaches out over people and conditions, controlling this situation and protecting my interests.*

This brings a picture of a long arm symbolizing strength and protection. With the realization of the power of the long arm of God, you would no longer resist or resent. You would relax and let go. The enemy thoughts within you would be destroyed, therefore, *the adverse conditions would disappear.*

Spiritual development means the ability to stand still, or stand aside, and let Infinite Intelligence lift your burdens and fight your battles. When the burden of resentment is lifted, you experience a sense of relief! You have a kindly feeling for everyone, and all the organs of your body begin to function properly.

A clipping quoting Albert Edward Day, D.D. reads, "That loving our enemies is good for our spiritual health is widely known and accepted. But that negation and poisonous emotions destroy

physical health, is a relatively new discovery. The problem of health is often an emotional one. Wrong emotions entertained and repeated are potent causes of illness. When the preacher talks about loving your enemies, the man on the street is apt to dismiss the idea as unendurable and pious. But the fact is, the preacher is telling you something which is one of the first laws of hygiene, as well as ethics. No man even for his body's sake can afford to indulge in hatred. It is like repeated doses of poison. When you are urged to get rid of fear, you are not listening to a moon-struck idealist; rather you are hearing counsel that is as significant for health as advice about diet."

We hear so much about a balanced diet, but without a balanced mind you can't digest what you eat, calories or no calories.

Non-resistance is an art. When acquired, The World is Yours! So many people are trying to force situations. Your lasting good will never come through forcing personal will.

> "Flee from the things which flee from thee,
> Seek nothing, fortune seeketh thee.
> Behold his shadow on the floor!
> Behold him standing at the door!"

I do not know the author of these lines. Lovelock, the celebrated English athlete, was asked how to attain his speed and endurance in running. He replied, "Learn to relax." Let us attain this rest in action. He was most relaxed when running the fastest.

Your big opportunity and big success usually

slide in, when you least expect it. You have to let go long enough for the *great law of attraction to operate. You never saw a worried and anxious magnet.* It stands up straight and hasn't a care in the world, because it knows the needles can't help jumping to it. The things we rightly desire come to pass when we have taken the clutch off.

I say in my correspondence course, *"Do not let your heart's desire become a heart's disease." You are completely demagnetized when you desire something too intensely.* You worry, fear, and agonize. There is an occult law of indifference: "None of these things move me." *Your ships come in over a don't care sea.*

Many people in Truth antagonize friends, because they are too anxious for them to read the books and go to the lectures. They meet opposition.

A friend took my book, "The Game of Life and How to Play It" to her brother's house to read. The young men of the family refused to read it. No "nut stuff" for them. One of these young men drives a taxi cab. One night he drove a taxi which belonged to another man. In going over the car he found a book stuffed away somewhere. It was "The Game of Life and How to Play It." The next day he said to his aunt, "I found Mrs. Shinn's book in the taxi last night. I read it and it's great! There's a lot of good reading in it. Why doesn't she write another book?" God works in round-about ways, His wonders to perform.

I meet unhappy people and a few grateful and contented people. A man said to me one day, "I

have a great deal to be thankful for. I have good health, enough money and I'm still single!"

The eighty-ninth psalm is very interesting, for we find that two individuals take part; the man who sings the psalm (for all psalms are songs or poems), and the Lord God of Hosts answers him. It is a song of praise and thanksgiving, extolling the strong arm of God.

"I will sing of the mercies of the Lord forever!"

"O Lord God of Hosts, who is a strong Lord like unto thee?"

"Thou hast a mighty arm: strong is thy hand, and high is thy right hand."

Then the Lord of Hosts replies.

"With whom my hand shall be established: mine arm also shall strengthen him."

"My mercy will I keep for him for evermore, and my covenant shall stand fast with him."

We only hear the words "for evermore" in the bible and in fairy-tales. In the absolute, man is outside of time and space. His good is "from everlasting to everlasting." The fairy-tales came down from the old Persian legends which were founded upon Truth.

Aladdin and His Wonderful Lamp is the outpicturing of the Word. Aladdin rubbed the lamp and all his desires came to pass. Your word is your lamp. Words and thoughts are a form of radio activity and do not return void. A scientist has said that words are clothed in light. *You are continually reaping the fruits of your words.*

A friend in one of my meeting said that she had brought a man to my class who had been out of

work for a year or more. I gave the statement: *Now is the appointed time. Today is the day of my amazing good fortune.* It clicked in his consciousness. Soon after, he was given a position which paid him nine thousand dollars a year.

A woman told me that when I blessed the offering I said that each offering would return a thousandfold. She had put a dollar in the collection. She said with great realization, "That dollar is blessed and returns a thousand dollars." She received a thousand dollars a short time afterwards, in a most unexpected way.

Why do some people demonstrate this Truth so much more quickly than others? It is because they have the ears that hear. Jesus Christ tells the parable of the man who sowed the seed and it fell upon good ground. The seed is the word. I say, *"Listen for the statement that clicks; the statement that gives you realization. That statement will bear fruit."*

The other day I went into a shop where I know the employer quite well. I had given one of his employees an affirmation card. I said to him, jokingly, "I wouldn't waste an affirmation card on you. You wouldn't use it." He replied, "Oh, sure, give me one. I'll use it." The following week I gave him a card. Before I left he rushed up to me excitedly and said, "I made that statement and two new customers walked in." It was: "Now is the appointed time; today is the day of my amazing good fortune." It had clicked.

So many people use their words in exaggerated and reckless statements. I find a great deal of

material for my talks in the beauty parlor. A young girl wanted a magazine to read. She called to the operator, "Give me something terribly new and frightfully exciting." All she wanted was the latest moving picture magazine. You hear people say, "I wish something terribly exciting would happen." They are inviting some unhappy, but exciting, experience into their lives. Then they wonder why it happened to them.

There should be a chair of metaphysics in all colleges. *Metaphysics is the wisdom of the ages.* It is the ancient wisdom taught all through the centuries in India and Egypt and Greece. Hermes Trismegistus was a great teacher of Egypt. His teachings were closely guarded and have come down to us over ten centuries. He lived in Egypt in the days when the present race of men was in its infancy. But if you read the "Kybalion" carefully, you will find that he taught just what we are teaching today. He said that all mental states were accompanied by vibrations. You combine with what you vibrate to, so let us all now vibrate to success, happiness and abundance.

Now is the appointed time. Today is the day of my amazing good fortune.

THE FORK IN THE ROAD

"Choose you this day whom ye will serve." — Josh. 24:15.

Every day there is a necessity of choice (a fork in the road).

"Shall I do this, or shall I do that? Shall I go, or shall I stay?" Many people do not know what to do. They rush about letting other people make decisions for them, then regret having taken their advice.

There are others who carefully reason things out. They weigh and measure the situation like dealing in groceries, and are surprised when they fail to attain their goal.

There are still other people who follow the magic path of intuition and find themselves in their Promised Land in the twinkling of an eye.

Intuition is a spiritual faculty high above the reasoning mind, but on that path is all that you desire or require.

In my book "The Game of Life and How to Play It," I give many examples of success attained through using this marvelous faculty. I say also that prayer is telephoning to God and intuition is

42

God telephoning to you. (Correspondence Course.)

So choose ye this day to follow the magic path of intuition.

In my question and answer classes I tell you how to cultivate intuition.

In most people it is a faculty which has remained dormant. So we say, "Awake thou that sleepeth. Wake up to your leads and hunches. Wake up to the divinity within!"

Claude Bragdon said, "To live intuitively is to live fourth dimensionally."

Now it is necessary for you to make a decision, you face a fork in the road. *Ask for a definite unmistakable lead,* and you will receive it.

We find many events to interpret metaphysically in the Book of Joshua. "After the death of Moses, the divine command came to Joshua, 'Now therefore, arise, go over the Jordan, thou and all thy people, unto the land which I do give to them. Every place the sole of your feet shall tread upon; to you have I given it'."

The feet are the symbol of understanding, so it means metaphysically all that we understand stands under us in consciousness, and what is rooted there can never be taken from us.

For, the bible goes on to say: "There shall not any man be able to stand before thee all the days of thy life. . . . I will not fail thee, nor forsake thee. Only be thou strong and very courageous, that thou mayest observe to do according to all the law, which Moses my servant commanded thee:

turn not from it to the right hand or to the left, that thou mayest prosper whithersoever thou goest."

So we find we have success through being strong and very courageous in following spiritual law. We are back again to the "fork in the road" — the necessity of choice.

"Choose you this day whom ye will serve," the intellect or divine guidance.

A well-known man, who has become a great power in the financial world, said to a friend, "I always follow intuition and I am luck incarnate."

Inspiration (which is divine guidance) is the most important thing in life. People come to Truth meetings for inspiration. I find the right word will start divine activity operating in their affairs.

A woman came to me with a complication of affairs. I said to her, "Let God juggle the situation." It clicked. She took the affirmation, "I now let God juggle this situation." Almost immediately she rented a house, which had been vacant for a long time.

Let God juggle every situation, for when you try to juggle the situation, you drop all the balls.

In my question and answer classes, I would be asked, "How do you let God juggle a situation, and what do you mean when you say I should not juggle it?"

You juggle with the intellect. The intellect would say, "Times are hard, no activity in real estate. Don't expect anything until the Fall of 1958."

With spiritual law there is only the *now*. Before you call you are answered, for "time and space are but a dream," and *your blessing is there waiting for you to release it by faith and the word.*

"Choose you this day whom ye will serve," fear or faith.

In every act prompted by fear lies the germ of its own defeat.

It takes much strength and courage to trust God. We often trust him in little things, but when it comes to a big situation we feel we had better attend to it ourselves; then comes defeat and failure.

The following extract from a letter which I received from a woman in the West shows how conditions can change in the twinkling of an eye.

"I've had the pleasure of reading your wonderful book, 'The Game of Life and How to Play It.' I have four boys, ten, thirteen, fifteen and seventeen, and thought how wonderful for them to grasp it, in their early life, and be able to get things which are theirs by Divine Right.

"The lady who let me read her copy gave me other things to read, but it seemed when I picked this book up it was magnetic and I could not let go of it. After reading it I realized, I was trying to live Divinely but did not understand the law, or I would have been much further advanced.

"At first I thought it quite hard to find a place in the business world, after so many years of being a mother. But I got this statement, *'God makes a way where there is no way.'* And He did that very thing for me.

"I am grateful for my position, and smile when people say, 'How do you do it, manage four growing boys, a home, after all the times you have been hospitalized with such major operations, and none of your relatives near you?'"

I have that statement in my book, *"God makes a way where there is no way."*

God made a way for her in business when all her friends said it couldn't be done.

The average person will tell you almost anything can't be done.

I had an example of this the other day. In a shop I found a delightful little silver dripolator which would make just one cup of anything. I showed it to some friends with enthusiasm, thinking it so very cute, and one said, "It will never work." The other said, "If it belonged to me, I'd throw it away." I stood up for the little dripolator and said I knew it would work, which it did.

My friends were simply typical of the average person who says, "It can't be done."

All big ideas meet with opposition.

Do not let other people rock your boat.

Follow the path of wisdom and understanding, "and turn not from it to the right hand or to the left, that thou mayest prosper whithersoever thou goest."

In the thirteenth verse of the twenty-fourth chapter of Joshua, we read a remarkable statement: "And I have given you a land for which ye did not labour, and cities which ye built not, and ye dwell in them; of the vineyards and oliveyards which ye planted not, do ye eat."

This shows that man cannot *earn* anything, his blessings come as gifts. (Gifts lest any man shall boast.)

With the *realization of wealth,* we receive the gift of wealth.

With the *realization of success,* we receive the gift of success, for success and abundance are states of mind.

"For it is the Lord our God, he it is, that brought us up, and our fathers out of the land of Egypt, out of the house of bondage."

The land of Egypt stands for darkness—the house of bondage, where man is a slave to his doubts and fears, and beliefs in lack and limitation, the result of having followed the wrong fork in the road.

Misfortune is due to failure to stick to the things which spirit has revealed through intuition.

All big things have been accomplished by men who stuck to their big ideas.

Henry Ford was past middle age when the idea of the Ford car came to him. He had great difficulty in raising the money. His friends thought it was a crazy idea. His father said to him, tearfully, "Henry, why do you give up a good twenty-five dollar a week job in order to chase a crazy idea?" But no one could rock Henry Ford's boat.

So in order to come out of the land of Egypt, out of the house of bondage, we must make the right decisions.

Follow the right fork in the road. "Only be thou strong and very courageous, that thou mayest observe to do according to the law, which Moses my

servant commanded thee: turn not from it to the right hand nor to the left, that thou mayest prosper whithersoever thou goest."

So, as we reach the fork in the road today, let us fearlessly follow the voice of intuition.

The bible calls it "the still small voice."

"There came a voice behind me, saying, 'This is the way, walk ye in it'."

On this path is the good, already prepared for you.

You will find the "land for which ye did not labour, and cities which ye built not, and ye dwell in them; of the vineyards and oliveyards which ye planted not, do ye eat."

I am divinely led, I follow the right fork in the road. God makes a way where there is no way.

CROSSING YOUR RED SEA

"Speak unto the children of Israel that they go forward."
Ex. 14:15

One of the most dramatic stories in the bible is the episode of the children of Israel crossing the Red Sea.

Moses was leading them out of the land of Egypt where they were kept in bondage and slavery. They were being pursued by the Egyptians.

The children of Israel, like most people, did not enjoy trusting God; they did a lot of murmuring. They said to Moses: "Is not this the word that we did tell thee in Egypt, saying, Let us alone, that we may serve the Egyptians? For it had been better for us to serve the Egyptians, than that we should die in the wilderness."

"And Moses said unto the people, Fear ye not, stand still, and see the salvation of the Lord, which he will show to you today: for the Egyptians whom ye have seen today, ye shall see them again no more for ever."

"The Lord shall fight for you, and ye shall hold your peace."

We might say that Moses pounded faith into the children of Israel.

They preferred being slaves to their old doubts and fears (for Egypt stands for darkness), than to take the giant swing into faith, and pass through the wilderness to their Promised Land.

There is, indeed, a wilderness to pass through before your Promised Land is reached.

The old doubts and fears encamp round about you, but, there is always someone to tell you to go forward! There is always a Moses on your pathway. Sometimes it is a friend, sometimes intuition!

"And the Lord said to Moses, Wherefore criest thou unto me? Speak unto the children of Israel, that *they go forward!*"

"But lift thou up thy rod, and stretch out thine hand over the sea, and divide it: and the children of Israel shall go on dry ground through the midst of the sea."

"And Moses stretched out his hand over the sea; and the Lord caused the sea to go back by a strong east wind all that night, and made the sea dry land, and the waters were divided."

"And the children of Israel went into the midst of the sea upon the dry ground: and the waters were a wall unto them on their right hand, and on their left."

"And the Egyptians pursued, and went in after them to the midst of the sea, even all Pharaoh's horses, his chariots, and his horsemen.

"And the Lord said unto Moses, Stretch out thine hand over the sea, that the waters may come again upon the Egyptians, upon their chariots, and upon their horsemen."

"And Moses stretched forth his hand over the

sea, and the sea returned; and the Egyptians fled against it; and the Lord overthrew the Egyptians in the midst of the sea."

"And the waters returned, and covered the chariots, and the horsemen, and all the hosts of Pharaoh that came into the sea after them; there remained not so much as one of them."

Now remember, the bible is talking about the individual. It is talking about *your* wilderness, *your* Red Sea, and *your* Promised Land.

Each one of you has a Promised Land, a heart's desire, but you have been so enslaved by the Egyptians (your negative thoughts), it seems very far away, and too good to be true. You consider trusting God a very risky proposition. The wilderness might prove worse than the Egyptians.

And how do you know your Promised Land really exists?

The reasoning mind will always back up the Egyptians.

But sooner or later, something says, *"Go forward!"* It is usually circumstances — you are driven to it.

I give the example of a student.

She is a very marvelous pianist and had great success abroad. She came back with a book full of press clippings, and a happy heart.

A relative took an interest in her and said she would back her financially for a concert tour. They chose a manager who took charge of the expenses, and attended to her bookings.

After a concert or two, there were no more funds. The manager had taken them. My friend

was left stranded, desolate and disappointed. This was about the time that she came to me.

She hated the man, and it was making her ill. She had very little money and could afford only a cheerless room where her hands were often too cold to practice.

She was indeed, in bondage to the Egyptians — hate, resentment, lack and limitation.

Someone brought her to one of my meetings, and she spoke to me and told her story.

I said, "In the first place you must stop hating that man. When you are able to forgive him, your success will come back to you. You are taking your initiation in forgiveness."

It seemed a pretty big order, but she tried and came regularly to all my meetings.

In the meantime, the relative had started a suit to recover the money. Time went on and it never came to court.

My friend had a call to go to California. She was no longer disturbed by the situation, and had forgiven the man.

Suddenly, after about four years, she was notified that the case had come to court. She called me upon her arrival in New York, and asked me to speak the word for rightness and justice.

They went at the time appointed, and it was all settled out of court, the man restoring the money by monthly payments.

She came to me overflowing with joy, for she said, "I hadn't the least resentment toward the man. He was amazed when I greeted him cordially." Her relative said that all the money was to

go to her, so she found herself with a big bank account.

Now she will soon reach her Promised Land. She came out of the house of bondage (of hate and resentment) and crossed her red sea. Her goodwill toward the man caused the waters to part, and she crossed over on dry land.

Dry land symbolizes something substantial under your feet, the feet symbolizing understanding.

Moses stands out as one of the greatest figures in biblical history.

"It came to Moses to move from Egypt with his nation. The task before him was not only the unwillingness of Pharaoh to let go of those whom he had made into profitable slaves, but also to stimulate to open rebellion this nation which had lost its initiative under the hardships of its taskmasters."

"It required extraordinary genius to meet this condition, which Moses possessed with self abnegation and the courage of his own convictions. Self abnegation! He was called the meekest of men. We have often heard the expression, 'As meek as Moses.' He was so meek towards the commands of the Lord, that he became one of the strongest of men."

The Lord said to Moses, "lift thou up thy rod, and stretch out thine hand over the sea, and divide it: and the children of Israel shall go on dry ground through the midst of the sea."

So, never doubting, he said to the children of Israel, "Go forward." This was a daring thing to do, to lead a multitude of people into the sea, having perfect faith they would not drown.

Behold the miracle!

". . . the Lord caused the sea to go back by a strong east wind all that night, and made the sea dry land, and the waters were divided."

Now remember, this could happen *for you* this very day. Think of your problem.

Maybe you have lost your initiative from living so long a slave to Pharaoh—(your doubts, fears and discouragements).

Say to yourself, *"Go forward."*

". . . the Lord caused the sea to go back by a strong east wind."

We will think of this strong east wind as a strong affirmation.

Take a vital statement of Truth. For example, if your problem is a financial one, say: *"My supply comes from God, and big happy financial surprises now come to me, under grace, in perfect ways."* The statement is a good one, for it contains the element of mystery.

We are told that God works in mysterious ways His wonders to perform. We might say in surprising ways. Now that you have made your statement for supply, you have caused the east wind to blow.

So walk up to your Red Sea of lack or limitation. The way to walk up to your Red Sea is to do something to *show* your fearlessness.

I will tell the story of a student who had an invitation to visit friends at a very fashionable summer resort.

She had been living in the country for a long time, grown heavier, and nothing fitted her but her girl scout suit. Suddenly, she received the invitation. It meant evening clothes, slippers and

accessories, none of which she had, and no money to buy them. She came to me. I said, "What is your hunch?"

She replied, "I feel very fearless. I have the hunch to go, anyway."

So she squeezed herself into something to travel in, and went.

When she arrived at her friend's house she was greeted warmly, but her hostess said, with some embarrassment, "Maybe what I've done will hurt you, but there are some evening clothes and slippers I never wear which I have put in your room. Won't you make use of them?"

My friend assured her she would be delighted— and everything fitted perfectly.

She had, indeed, walked up to her Red Sea and passed over on dry land.

The waters of my Red Sea part, and I pass over on dry land, I now go forward into my Promised Land.

THE WATCHMAN AT THE GATE

"Also I set watchmen over you, saying, Hearken to the sound of the trumpet." — Jeremiah 6:17

We must all have a watchman at the gate of our thoughts. The Watchman at the Gate is the super-conscious mind.

We have the power to choose our thoughts.

Since we have lived in the race thought for thousands of years, it seems almost impossible to control them. They rush through our minds like stampeding cattle or sheep.

But a single sheep-dog can control the frightened sheep and guide them into the sheep pen.

I saw a picture in the news-reels of a shepherd-dog controlling the sheep. He had rounded up all but three. These three resisted and resented. They baahed and lifted their front feet in protest, but the dog simply sat down in front and never took his eyes off them. He did not bark or threaten. He just sat and looked his determination. In a little while the sheep tossed their heads and went in the pen.

We can learn to control our thoughts in the same way, by gentle determination, not force.

We take an affirmation and repeat it continually, while our thoughts are on the rampage.

We cannot always control our thoughts, but we *can control our words,* and repetition impresses the subconscious, and we are then master of the situation.

In the sixth chapter of Jeremiah we read: "I set a watchman over you, saying, Hearken to the sound of the trumpet."

Your success and happiness in life depend upon the watchman at the gate of your thoughts, for your thoughts, sooner or later, crystallize on the external.

People think by running away from a negative situation, they will be rid of it, but the same situation confronts them wherever they go.

They will meet the same experiences until they have learned their lessons. This idea is brought out in the moving picture, "The Wizard of Oz."

The little girl, Dorothy, is very unhappy because the mean woman in the village wants to take away her dog, Toto.

She goes, in despair, to confide in her Aunt Em and Uncle Henry, but they are too busy to listen, and tell her to "run along."

She says to Toto, "There is somewhere, a wonderful place high above the skies where everybody is happy and no one is mean." How she would love to be there!

A Kansas cyclone suddenly comes along, and she and Toto are lifted up, high in the sky, and land in the country of Oz.

Everything seems very delightful at first, but soon she has the same old experiences. The mean old woman of the village has turned into a terrible witch, and is still trying to get Toto from her.

How she wishes she were back in Kansas.

She is told to find the Wizard of Oz. He is all powerful and will grant her request.

She starts off to find his palace in the Emerald City.

On the way she meets a scarecrow. He is so unhappy because he hasn't a brain.

She meets a man made of tin, who is so unhappy because he hasn't a heart.

Then she meets a lion who is so unhappy because he has no courage.

She cheers them up by saying, "We'll all go to the Wizard of Oz and he'll give us what we want" —the scarecrow a brain, the tin man a heart, and the lion courage.

They encounter terrible experiences, for the bad witch is determined to capture Dorothy and take away Toto and the ruby slippers which protect her.

At last they reach the Emerald Palace of the Wizard of Oz.

They ask for an audience, but are told no one has ever seen the Wizard of Oz, who lives mysteriously in the palace.

But through the influence of the good witch of the North, they enter the palace. There they discover that the Wizard is just a fake magician from Dorothy's home town in Kansas.

They are all in despair because their wishes cannot be granted!

But then the good witch shows them that their wishes are *already* granted. The scarecrow has developed a brain by having to decide what to do

in the experiences he has encountered, the tin man finds he has a heart because he loves Dorothy, and the lion has become courageous because he *had* to show courage in his many adventures.

The good witch from the North says to Dorothy, "What have you learned from your experiences?" and Dorothy replies, "I have learned that my heart's desire is in my own home and in my own front yard." So the good witch waves her wand, and Dorothy is at home again.

She wakes up and finds that the scarecrow, the tin man, and the lion are the men who work on her uncle's farm. They are so glad to have her back. This story teaches *that if you run away your problems will run after you.*

Be *undisturbed* by a situation, and it will fall away of its own weight.

There is an occult law of indifference. "None of these things moves me." "None of these things disturbs me;" we might say in modern language.

When you can no longer be disturbed, all disturbance will disappear from the external.

"When your eyes have seen your teachers, your teachers disappear."

"I set watchmen over you, saying, Hearken to the sound of the trumpet."

A trumpet is a musical instrument, used in olden times, to draw people's attention to something; to victory, to order.

You will form the habit of giving attention to every thought and word, when you realize their importance.

The imagination, the scissors of the mind, is

constantly cutting out the events to come into your life.

Many people are cutting out fear-pictures. Seeing things which are not divinely planned.

With the "single eye," man sees only the Truth. He sees through evil, knowing that out of it comes good. He transmutes injustice into justice, and disarms his seeming enemy by sending *goodwill.*

We read in mythology of the Cyclops, a race of giants, said to have inhabited Sicily. These giants had only one eye in the middle of the forehead.

The seat of the imagining faculty is situated in the forehead (between the eyes). So these fabled giants came from this idea.

You are indeed a giant when you have a single eye. Then every thought will be a constructive thought, and every word, a word of Power.

Let the third eye be the watchman at the gate.

"If therefore thine eye be single, thy whole body is full of light."

With the single eye your body will be transformed into your spiritual body, the "body electric" made in God's likeness and image (imagination).

By seeing clearly the perfect plan, we could redeem the world: with our *inner eye* seeing a world of peace and plenty and good will.

"Judge not by appearances, judge righteous judgment."

"Nation shall not lift up sword against nation, neither shall they learn war anymore."

The occult law of indifference means that you

are undisturbed by adverse appearances. You hold steadily to the *constructive thought, which wins out.*

Spiritual law transcends the law of Karma.

This is the attitude of mind which must be held by the healer or practitioner towards his patient.

Indifferent to appearances of lack, loss or sickness, he brings about the change in mind, body and affairs.

Let me quote from the thirty-first chapter of Jeremiah. The keynote is one of rejoicing. It gives a picture of the individual freed from negative thinking.

"For there shall be a day that the watchmen upon the mount Ephraim shall cry, Arise ye, and let us go up to Zion unto the Lord our God."

The Watchman at the Gate neither slumbers nor sleeps. It is the "eye which watches over Israel."

But the individual, living in a world of negative thought, is not conscious of this inner eye.

He may occasionally have flashes of intuition or illumination, then falls back into a world of chaos.

It takes determination and eternal vigilance to check up on words and thoughts. Thoughts of fear, failure, resentment and ill-will must be dissolved and dissipated.

Take the statement: "Every plant my father in heaven has not planted shall be rooted up."

This gives you a vivid picture of rooting up weeds in a garden. They are thrown aside, and dry up because they are without soil to nourish them.

You nourish negative thoughts by giving them your attention. Use the occult law of indifference and refuse to be interested.

Soon you will starve out the "army of the aliens." Divine ideas will crowd your consciousness, false ideas fade away, and you will desire only that which God desires through you.

The Chinese have a proverb, "The Philosopher leaves the cut of his coat to the tailor."

So leave the plan of your life to the Divine Designer, and you will find all conditions permanently perfect.

The ground I am on is holy ground. I now expand rapidly into the divine plan of my life, where all conditions are permanently perfect.

THE WAY OF ABUNDANCE

"Then shalt thou lay up gold as dust." — Job 22:24

The way of abundance is a one-way street.

As the old saying is, "there are no two ways about it."

You are either heading for lack, or heading for abundance. The man with a rich consciousness and the man with a poor consciousness are not walking on the same mental street.

There is a lavish supply, divinely planned for each individual.

The rich man is tapping it, for rich thoughts produce rich surroundings.

Change your thoughts, and in the twinkling of an eye, all your conditions change. Your world is a world of crystallized ideas, crystallized words.

Sooner or later, you reap the fruits of your words and thoughts.

"Words are bodies or forces which move spirally and return in due season to cross the lives of their creators." People who are always talking lack and limitation, reap lack and limitation.

You cannot enter the Kingdom of Abundance bemoaning your lot.

I know a woman who had always been limited in her ideas of prosperity. She was continually making her old clothes "do," instead of buying new clothes. She was very careful of what money she had, and was always advising her husband not to spend so much. She said repeatedly, "I don't want anything I can't afford."

She couldn't afford much, so she didn't have much. Suddenly her whole world cracked up. Her husband left her, weary of her nagging and limited thoughts. She was in despair, when one day she came across a book on metaphysics. It explained the power of thought and words.

She realized that she had invited every unhappy experience by wrong thinking. She laughed heartily at her mistakes, and decided to profit by them. She determined *to prove the law of abundance.*

She used what money she had, fearlessly, to show her faith in her invisible supply. She relied upon God as the source of her prosperity. She no longer voiced lack and limitation. She kept herself feeling and looking prosperous.

Her old friends scarcely recognized her. She had swung into the way of abundance. More money came to her than she had ever had before. Unheard-of doors opened — amazing channels were freed. She became very successful in a work she had had no training for.

She found herself on *miracle ground.* What had happened?

She had changed the quality of her words and thoughts. She had taken God into her confidence, and into all her affairs. She had many eleventh-

hour demonstrations, but her supply always came, for she dug her ditches and gave thanks without wavering.

Someone called me up recently and said, "I am looking desperately for a position."

I replied, "Don't look desperately for it, look for it with praise and thanksgiving, for Jesus Christ, the greatest of metaphysicians, said to pray with praise and thanksgiving."

Praise and thanksgiving open the gates, for expectancy always wins.

Of course, the law is impersonal, and a dishonest person with rich thoughts will attract riches— but, "a thing ill-got has ever bad success," as Shakespeare says. It will be of short duration and will not bring happiness.

We have only to read the papers to see that the way of the transgressor is hard.

That is the reason it is so necessary to make your demands aright on the Universal Supply, and ask for what is yours by divine right and under grace in a perfect way.

Some people attract prosperity, but cannot hold it. Sometimes their heads are turned, sometimes they lose it through fear and worry.

A friend in one of my question and answer classes told this story.

Some people in his home town, who had always been poor, suddenly struck oil in their back yard. It brought great riches. The father joined the country club and went in for golf. He was no longer young—the exercise was too much for him and he dropped dead on the links.

This filled the whole family with fear. They all

decided they might have heart trouble, so they are now in bed with trained nurses watching every heart beat.

In the race-thought people must worry about something.

They no longer worried about money, so they shifted their worries to health.

The old idea was, "that you can't have everything." If you got one thing, you'd lose another. People were always saying, "Your luck won't last," "It's too good to be true."

Jesus Christ said, "In the world (world thought) there is tribulation, but be of good cheer, I have overcome the world (thought)."

In the superconscious (or Christ within), there is a lavish supply for every demand, and your good is perfect and permanent.

"If thou return to the Almighty, thou shalt be built up (in consciousness), thou shalt put away iniquity far from thy tabernacles."

"Then shalt thou lay up gold as dust, the gold of Ophir as the stones of the brooks."

"Yea, the Almighty shall be thy defense and thou shalt have plenty of silver."

What a picture of opulence! The result of "Returning to the Almighty (in consciousness)."

With the average person (who has thought in terms of lack for a long time) it is very difficult to build up a rich consciousness.

I have a student who has attracted great success by making the statement: *"I am the daughter of the King! My rich Father now pours out his abundance upon me: I am the daughter of the King! Everything makes way for me."*

Many people put up with limited conditions because they are too lazy (mentally), to think themselves out of them.

You must have a great desire for financial freedom, you must feel yourself rich, you must see yourself rich, you must continually prepare for riches. Become as a little child and make believe you are rich. You are then impressing the subconscious with expectancy.

The imagination is man's workshop, the scissors of the mind, where he is constantly cutting out the events of his life!

The superconscious is the realm of inspiration, revelation, illumination and intuition.

Intuition is usually known as a hunch. I do not apologize for the word "hunch" anymore. It is now in Webster's latest dictionary.

I had a hunch to look up "hunch," and there it was.

The superconscious is the realm of perfect ideas. The great genius captures his thoughts from the superconscious.

"Without the vision (imagination) my people perish."

When people have lost the power to image their good, they "perish" (or go under).

It is interesting to compare the translation of the French and English Bibles. In the 21st verse of the 22nd chapter of Job we read: "Acquaint now thyself with him, and be at peace: thereby good shall come unto thee." In the French Bible we read: "Attach thyself to God and you will have peace. Thou shalt thus enjoy happiness."

The 23rd verse: "If thou return to the Almighty,

thou shalt be built up, thou shalt put away iniquity far from thy tabernacles." In the French translation we read: "Thou shalt be re-established if thou returnest to the Almighty, putting iniquity far off from your dwellings."

In the 24th verse we read a new and amazing translation. The English Bible reads: "Then shalt thou lay up gold as dust, and the gold of Ophir as the stones of the brooks." The French Bible says: "Throw gold into the dust, the gold of Ophir amongst the pebbles of the torrents; and the Almighty shall be thy gold, thy silver, thy riches."

This means if people are depending entirely on their visible supply, it is even better to throw it away and trust absolutely to the Almighty for gold, silver and riches.

I give an example in the story told me by a friend.

A priest went to visit a nunnery in France, where they fed many children. One of the nuns, in despair, told the priest they had no food; the children must go hungry. She said that they had but one piece of silver (about the value of a quarter of a dollar). They needed food and clothing.

The priest said, "Give me the coin."

She handed it to him and he threw it out the window.

"Now," he said, "rely entirely upon God."

Within a short time friends arrived with plenty of food and gifts of money.

This does not mean to throw away what money you have, but don't depend upon it. *Depend upon your invisible supply, the Bank of the Imagination.*

Let us now attach ourselves to God and have peace. For He shall be our gold, our silver and our riches.

The inspiration of the Almighty shall be my defense and I shall have plenty of silver.

I SHALL NEVER WANT

"The Lord is my Shepherd; I shall not want." — Psalms 23:1

The 23rd Psalm is the best known of all the Psalms — we might say that it is the keynote to the message of the Bible.

It tells man he shall never want, when he has the realization (or conviction) that the Lord is his Shepherd: the *realization* that Infinite Intelligence supplies every need.

If you get this conviction today, every need will be met now and forever-more; you will draw, instantly, from the abundance of the spheres, whatever you desire or require; for what you need is *already on your pathway.*

A woman suddenly had the realization: "The Lord is my Shepherd, I shall never want." She seemed to be touching her invisible supply, she felt outside of Time and Space, she no longer relied on the external.

Her first demonstration was a small, but necessary one. She needed at once, some large paper-clips, but had no time to go to a stationer's to buy them.

In looking for something else, she opened a

little-used chest, and in it, she found, about a dozen large paper-clips. She felt that the law was working, and gave thanks; then some needed money appeared, things large and small came her way.

Since then she has relied upon the statement: "The Lord is my Shepherd, I shall never want."

We used to hear people say, "I do not think it is right to ask God for money or things."

They did not realize that this Creative Principle is within each man.—(The Father within). True Spirituality is proving God as your supply, daily—not just once in a while.

Jesus Christ knew this law, for whatever He desired or required, appeared immediately on His pathway, the loaves and fishes and money from the fish's mouth.

With this realization, all hoarding and saving would disappear.

This does not mean that you should not have a big bank account, and investments, but it does mean that you should not depend upon them, for if you had a loss in one direction, you would have a gain in another.

Always "your barns would be full and your cup flow over."

Now, how does one make this contact with his invisible supply? By taking a statement of Truth which clicks and gives him realization.

This is not open to a chosen few, "Whosoever calleth on the name of the Lord shall be delivered." The Lord is *your* shepherd and *my* shepherd and *everybody's* shepherd.

God is the Supreme Intelligence devoted to supplying man's need; the explanation is, that man is God in action. Jesus Christ said, "I and the Father are one."

We might paraphrase the statement and say, I and the great Creative Principle of the Universe, are one and the same.

Man only lacks when he loses his contact with this Creative Principle, which must be fully trusted, for it is Pure Intelligence and knows the way of Fulfillment.

The reasoning mind and personal will, cause a short circuit.

"Trust in me and I will bring it to pass."

Most people are filled with apprehension and dread, when there is nothing to cling to on the external.

A woman came to a practitioner and said, "I'm only a poor little woman with no one but God back of me." The practitioner said, — "You need not worry if you have God back of you," for "all that the Kingdom affords is yours."

A woman called me on the phone and said, almost in tears, "I'm so worried about the business situation." I replied, "The situation with God remains the same: The Lord is your Shepherd: you shall not want." "If one door shuts, another door opens."

A very successful business-man who conducts all affairs on Truth methods, said, "The trouble with most people is, that they get to relying on certain conditions. They haven't enough imagination to go forward — to open new channels."

Nearly every big success is built upon a failure.

I was told that Edgar Bergen lost his part in a Broadway production because they did not want any more dummies. Noel Coward got him on the Rudy Vallee radio hour, and he and Charlie McCarthy became famous over night.

I told the story, at one of my meetings, of a man who was so poor and discouraged, that he ended it all. A few days later, came a letter notifying him that he had inherited a large fortune.

A man in the meeting said: "That means, when you want to be dead, your demonstration is three days off." Yes, *do not be fooled by the darkness before the dawn.*

It is a good thing to see the dawn once in a while, to convince you how unfailing it is. It reminds me of an experience of several years ago.

I had a friend who lived in Brooklyn near Prospect Park. She liked to do unusual things and said to me: "Come to visit me and we'll get up early and see the sun-rise in Prospect Park."

At first I refused, and then came the hunch that it would be an interesting experience.

It was in the summer. We got up about four o'clock, — my friend, her little daughter and myself. It was pitch dark, but we sallied forth down the street, to the entrance of the Park.

Some policemen eyed us curiously, but my friend said to them with dignity, "We are going to see the sun-rise;" and it seemed to satisfy them. We walked through the Park to the beautiful rose-garden.

A faint pink streak appeared in the East, then

suddenly, we heard a most tremendous uproar. We were near the Zoo and all the animals were greeting the dawn.

The lions and tigers roared, the hyenas laughed, there were shrieks and howls: every animal had something to say, for a new day was at hand.

It was indeed, most inspiring. The light slanted through the trees; everything had an unearthly aspect.

Then, as it grew lighter, our shadows were in front instead of behind us. The dawn of a new day!

This is the wonderful dawn which comes to each one of us, after some darkness.

Your dawn of Success, Happiness and Abundance is sure to come.

Every day is important, for we read in the wonderful Sanskrit poem, "Look well, therefore, to this day, such is the salutation of the dawn."

This day the Lord is your Shepherd! *This day,* you shall not want; as you and this great Creative Principle are one and the same.

The 34th Psalm is also a Psalm of security. It starts with a blessing for the Lord, "I will bless the Lord at all times: His praise shall continually be in my mouth."

"They that seek the Lord shall not want any good thing." Seeking the Lord means that man must make the first move. "Draw near to me and I will draw near to thee, saith the Lord."

You seek the Lord by making your affirmation, expecting and preparing for your good.

If you ask for success and prepare for failure, you will receive the thing you have prepared for.

I tell in my book, "The Game of Life and How to Play It," of a man who asked me to speak the word that all his debts be wiped out.

After the treatment, he said, "Now I'm thinking what I'll say to the people when I haven't the money to pay them." A treatment won't help you if you haven't faith in it, for faith and expectancy impress the subconscious mind with the picture of fulfillment.

In the 23rd Psalm we read, "He restoreth my soul." Your soul is your subconscious mind and must be re-stored with the right ideas.

Whatever you feel deeply is impressed upon the subconscious, and manifests in your affairs.

If you are convinced that you are a failure, you will be a failure, until you impress the subconscious with the conviction you are a success.

This is done by making an affirmation which "clicks."

A friend in a meeting said that I had given her the statement as she was leaving the room — *"The ground you are on is harvest ground."* Things with her, had been very dull; but this statement clicked.

"Harvest Ground, Harvest Ground," rang in her ears. Good things immediately commenced to come to her, and happy surprises.

The reason it is necessary to make an affirmation is because repetition impresses the subconscious. You cannot control your thoughts at first, but you can control your words, and Jesus Christ

said: "By your *words* you are justified and by your *words* you are condemned."

Every day, choose the right words; the right thoughts!

The Imaging faculty is the creative faculty: "Out of the imaginations of the heart come the issues of life."

We have all a bank we can draw upon, the Bank of the Imagination.

Let us imagine ourselves rich, well and happy: imagine all our affairs in divine order; but leave the way of fulfillment to Infinite Intelligence.

"He has weapons ye know not of," He has channels which will surprise you.

One of the most important passages in the 23rd Psalm is—"Thou preparest a table before me in the presence of mine enemies."

This means that even in the presence of the enemy situation, brought on by your doubts, fears or resentments, a way out is prepared for you.

The Lord is my Shepherd; I shall never want.

LOOK WITH WONDER

"I will remember the works of the Lord; surely I will remember thy wonders of old." — Psalms 77:11

The words wonder and wonderful are used many times in the Bible. In the dictionary the word wonder is defined as, "a cause for surprise, astonishment, a miracle, a marvel."

Ouspensky, in his book, "Tertium Organum," calls the 4th dimensional world, the "World of the Wondrous." He has figured out mathematically, that there is a realm where all conditions are perfect. Jesus Christ called it the Kingdom.

We might say, "Seek ye first the world of the wondrous, and all things shall be added unto you."

It can only be reached through a state of consciousness.

Jesus Christ said, to enter the Kingdom, we must become "as a little child." Children are continually in a state of joy and wonder!

The future holds promises of mysterious good. Anything can happen over night.

Robert Louis Stevenson, in "A Child's Garden of Verses" says: "The world is so full of a number

of things, I'm sure we should all be as happy as kings."

So let us look with wonder at that which is before us; that statement was given me a number of years ago, I mention it in my book, "The Game of Life and How To Play It."

I had missed an opportunity and felt that I should have been more awake to my good. The next day, I took the statement early in the morning, "I look with wonder at that which is before me."

At noon the phone rang, and the proposition was put to me again. This time I grasped it: I did indeed, look with wonder for I never expected the opportunity to come to me again.

A friend in one of my meetings said the other day, that this statement had brought her wonderful results. It fills the consciousness with happy expectancy.

Children are filled with happy expectancy until grown-up people, and unhappy experiences bring them out of the world of the wondrous!

Let us look back and remember some of the gloomy ideas which were given us: "Eat the speckled apples first." "Don't expect too much, then you won't be disappointed." "You can't have everything in this life." "Childhood is your happiest time." "No one knows what the future will bring." What a start in life!

These are some of the impressions I picked up in early childhood.

At the age of six I had a great sense of responsibility. Instead of looking with wonder at that

which was before me, I looked with fear and suspicion. I feel much younger now than I did when I was six.

I have an early photograph taken about that time, grasping a flower, but with a careworn and hopeless expression.

I had left the world of the wondrous behind me! I was now living in the world of realities, as my elders told me, and it was far from wondrous.

It is a great privilege for children to live in this age, when they are taught Truth from their birth. Even if they are not taught actual metaphysics, the ethers are filled with joyous expectancy.

You may become a Shirley Temple or a Freddy Bartholomew or a great pianist at the age of six, and go on a concert tour.

We are all now, back in the world of the wondrous, where anything can happen over-night, for when miracles do come, they come quickly!

So let us become *Miracle Conscious:* prepare for miracles, expect miracles, and we are then inviting them into our lives.

Maybe you need a financial miracle! There is a supply for every demand. Through active faith, the word, and intuition, we release this invisible supply.

I will give an example: One of my students found herself almost without funds, she needed one thousand dollars, and she had had plenty of money at one time and beautiful possessions, but had nothing left but an ermine wrap. No fur dealer would give her much for it.

I spoke the word that it would be sold to the

right person for the right price, or that the supply would come in some other way. It was necessary that the money manifest at once, it was no time to worry or reason.

She was on the street making her affirmations. It was a stormy day—She said to herself, "I'm going to show active faith in my invisible supply by taking a taxi cab:" it was a very strong hunch. As she got out of the taxi, at her destination, a woman stood waiting to get in.

It was an old friend: a very very kind friend. It was the first time in her life she had ever taken a taxi, but her Rolls Royce was out of commission that afternoon.

They talked, and my friend told her about the ermine wrap; "Why," her friend said, "I will give you a thousand dollars for it." And that afternoon she had the cheque.

God's ways are ingenious, His methods are sure.

A student wrote me the other day, that she was using that statement—*God's ways are ingenious, His methods are sure.* A series of unexpected contacts brought about a situation she had been desiring. She looked with wonder at the working of the law.

Our demonstrations usually come within a "split second." All is timed with amazing accuracy in Divine Mind.

My student left the taxi, just as her friend stopped to enter; a second later, she would have hailed another taxi.

Man's part is to be wide awake to his leads and

hunches; for on the magic path of Intuition is all that he desires or requires.

In Moulton's Modern Reader's Bible, the book of Psalms is recognized as the perfection of lyric poetry.

"The musical meditation which is the essence of lyrics can find no higher field than the devout spirit which at once raises itself to the service of God, and overflows on the various sides of active and contemplative life."

The Psalms are also human documents, and I have selected the 77th Psalm because it gives the picture of a man in despair, but as he contemplates the wonders of God, faith and assurance are restored to him.

"I cried unto God with my voice, even unto God with my voice; and He gave ear unto me.

In the day of my trouble I sought the Lord: my soul refused to be comforted.

Will the Lord cast off forever? and will he be favourable no more?

Hath God forgotten to be gracious? hath he in anger shut up his tender mercies?

And I said, This is my infirmity: but I will remember the years of the right hand of the Most High.

I will remember the works of the Lord; surely I will remember thy wonders of old.

I will meditate also of all thy work, and talk of thy doings.

Thy way, O God, is in the sanctuary: who is so great a God as our God!

Thou art the God that doest wonders.

Thou hast with thine arm redeemed thy people."

This is a picture of what the average Truth student goes through, when confronted with a problem; he is assailed by thoughts of doubt, fear and despair.

Then some statement of Truth will flash into his consciousness—"God's ways are ingenious, His methods are sure!"—He remembers other difficulties which have been overcome, his confidence in God returns. He thinks, *"what God has done before, He will do for me and more!"*

I was talking to a friend not long ago who said: "I would be pretty dumb if I didn't believe God could solve my problem. So many times before, wonderful things have come to me, I know they will come again!"

So the summing up of the 77th Psalm is, "What God has done before, He now does for me and more!"

It is a good thing to say when you think of your past success, happiness or wealth: all loss comes from your own vain imaginings, fear of loss crept into your consciousness, you carried burdens and fought battles, you reasoned instead of sticking to the magic path of intuition.

But in the twinkling of an eye, all will be restored to you—for as they say in the East—"What Allah has given, cannot be diminished."

Now to go back to the child's state of consciousness, you should be filled with wonder, but be careful not to live in your past childhood.

I know people who can only think about their happy childhood days: they remember what they wore! No skies have since been so blue, or grass so green. They therefore miss the opportunities of the wonderful now.

I will tell an amusing story of a friend who lived in a town when she was very young, then moved away to another city. She always looked back to the house they first lived in; to her it was an enchanted palace: large, spacious and glamorous.

Many years after, when she had grown up, she had an opportunity of visiting this house. She was disillusioned: she found it small, stuffy and ugly. Her idea of beauty had entirely changed, for in the front yard was an iron dog.

If you went back to your past, it would not be the same. So in this friend's family, they called living in the past, "iron-dogging."

Her sister told me a story of some "iron-dogging" she had done. When she was about sixteen, she met abroad, a very dashing and romantic young man, an artist. This romance didn't last long, but she talked about it a lot to the man she afterwards married.

Years rolled by, the dashing and romantic young man, had become a well-known artist; and came to this country to have an exhibition of his pictures. My friend was filled with excitement, and hunted him up to renew their friendship. She went to his exhibition, and in walked a portly business man—no trace was left of the dashing romantic youth! When she told her husband, all he said was, "iron-dogging."

Remember, *now* is the appointed time! *Today* is the day! *And your good can happen over night.*

Look with wonder at that which is before you!

We are filled with divine expectancy: "I will restore to you the years which the locusts have eaten!"

Now let each one think of the good which seems so difficult to attain; it may be health, wealth, happiness or perfect self-expression.

Do not think *how* your good can be accomplished, just give thanks that you have already received on the invisible plane, "therefore the steps leading up to it are secured also."

Be wide awake to your intuitive leads, and suddenly, you find yourself in your Promised Land.

"I look with wonder at that which is before me."

CATCH UP WITH YOUR GOOD

"And it shall come to pass, that before they call, I will answer: and while they are yet speaking, I will hear."

—Isaiah 65:24

Catch up with your good! This is a new way of saying, "Before they call, I will answer."

Your good *precedes* you; it gets there before you do. But how to catch up with your good? For you must have ears that hear, and eyes that see, or it will escape you.

Some people never catch up with their good in life; they will say, "My life has always been one of hardship, no good luck ever comes to me." They are the people who have been asleep to their opportunities; or through laziness, haven't caught up with their good.

A woman told a group of friends that she had not eaten for three days. They dashed about asking people to give her work; but she refused it. She explained that she never got up until twelve o'clock, she liked to lie in bed and read magazines.

She just wanted people to support her while she read "Vogue" and "Harper's Bazaar." We must be careful not to slip into lazy states of mind.

Take the affirmation, *I am wide awake to my good, I never miss a trick.* Most people are only half awake to their good.

A student said to me, "If I don't follow my hunches, I always get into a jam."

I will tell the story of a woman, one of my students, who followed her intuitive lead, which brought amazing results.

She had been asked to visit friends in a nearby town. She had very little money. When she arrived at her destination, she found the house locked up, they had gone away: she was filled with despair, then commenced to pray: she said, "Infinite Intelligence, give me a definite lead, let me know just what to do!"

The name of a certain hotel flashed into her consciousness—it persisted—the name seemed to stand out in big letters.

She had just enough money to get back to New York and the hotel. As she was about to enter, an old friend suddenly appeared, who greeted her warmly; and whom she hadn't seen for years.

She explained that she was living at the hotel but was going away for several months, and added, "Why don't you live in my suite while I am away: —it won't cost you a cent."

My friend accepted gratefully, and looked with amazement on the working of Spiritual law.

She had caught up with her good by following intuition.

All going forward comes from desire. Science today, is going back to Lamarck and his "dint—of wishing" theory. He claims that birds do not fly

because they have wings, but they have wings because they wanted to fly; result of the "Push of the emotional wish."

Think of the irresistible power of thought with clear vision. Many people are in a fog most of the time, making wrong decisions and going the wrong way.

During the Christmas rush, my maid said to a saleswoman at one of the big shops, "I suppose this is your busiest day." She replied, "Oh no! the day *after* Christmas is our busiest day, when people bring most of the things back."

Hundreds of people choosing the wrong gifts because they were not listening to their intuitive leads.

No matter what you are doing, ask for guidance. It saves time and energy and often a lifetime of misery.

All suffering comes from the violation of intuition. Unless intuition builds the house, they labor in vain who build it.

Get the *habit of hunching,* then you will always be on the magic path.

"And it shall come to pass, that before they call, I will answer: and while they are yet speaking, I will hear."

Working with spiritual law, we are bringing to pass that which already is. In the Universal Mind it is there as an idea, but is crystallized on the external, by a sincere desire.

The idea of a bird was a perfect picture in divine mind; the fish caught the idea, and wished themselves into birds.

Are your desires bringing you wings? *We should all be bringing some seemingly impossible thing to pass.*

One of my affirmations is, *"The unexpected happens, my seemingly impossible good now comes to pass."*

Do not magnify obstacles, magnify the Lord— that means, magnify God's power.

The average person will dwell on all the obstacles and hindrances which are there to prevent his good coming to pass.

You "combine with what you notice," so if you give obstacles and hindrances your undivided attention, they grow worse and worse.

Give God your undivided attention. Keep saying silently (in the face of all obstacles), *"God's ways are ingenious, His methods are sure."*

God's power is invincible, (though invisible). "Call unto me and I will answer thee, and show thee great and mighty things, which thou knowest not."

In demonstrating our good, we must look away from adverse appearances, "Judge not by appearances."

Get some statement which will give you a feeling of assurance, *The long arm of God reaches out over people and conditions, controlling the situation and protecting my interests!*

I was asked to speak the word for a man who was to have a business interview with a seemingly unscrupulous person. I used the statement, and rightness and justice came out of the situation, at just the exact time I was speaking.

We have all heard the quotation from Proverbs, "Hope deferred maketh the heart grow sick, but when the desire cometh, it is a tree of life."

In desiring sincerely (without anxiety), we are catching up with the thing desired; and the desire becomes crystallized on the external. "I will give to you the rightous desires of your heart."

Selfish desires, desires which harm others, always return to harm the sender.

The righteous desire might be called, an echo from the Infinite. It is already a perfect idea in divine mind.

All inventors catch up with the ideas of the articles they invent. I say in my book, "The Game of Life and How To Play It," the telephone was seeking Bell.

Often two people discover the same inventions at the same time; they have tuned in with the same idea.

The most important thing in life, is to bring the divine plan to pass.

Just as the picture of the oak is in the acorn, the divine design of your life is in your superconscious mind, and you must work out the perfect pattern in your affairs. You will then lead a magic life, for in the divine design, all conditions are permanently perfect.

People defy the divine design when they are asleep to their good.

Perhaps the woman who liked to lie in bed most of the day, and read magazines, should be writing for magazines, but her habits of laziness dulled all desire to go forward.

The fishes who desired wings, were alert and alive, they did not spend their days on the bed of the ocean, reading "Vogue" and "Harper's Bazaar."

Awake thou that sleepeth and catch up with your good!

"Call on me and I will answer thee, and show thee great and mighty things, which thou knowest not."

I now catch up with my good, for before I called I was answered.

RIVERS IN THE DESERT

"Behold, I will do a new thing: now it shall spring forth;
shall ye not know it? I will even make a way in the wilderness,
and rivers in the desert." — Isaiah 43:19.

In this 43rd chapter of Isaiah, are many wonderful statements, showing the irresistible power
of Supreme Intelligence, coming to man's rescue
in times of trouble. *No matter how impossible the
situation seems, Infinite Intelligence knows the
way out.*

Working with God-Power, man becomes
unconditioned and absolute. Let us get a realization of this hidden power we can call upon at any
moment.

Make your contact with Infinite Intelligence,
(the God within) and all appearance of evil evaporates, for it comes from man's "vain imaginings."

In my question and answer class I would be
asked, "How do you make a conscious contract
with this Invincible Power?"

I reply, "By your word." "By your word you are
justified."

The Centurion said to Jesus Christ, "Speak the
word master and my servant shall be healed."

"Whosoever calleth on the name of the Lord
shall be delivered." Notice the word, "call:" you

are calling on the Lord or Law, when you make an affirmation of Truth.

As I always say, take a statement which "clicks," that means, gives you a feeling of security.

People are enslaved by ideas of lack; lack of love, lack of money, lack of companionship, lack of health, and so on.

They are enslaved by the ideas of interference and incompletion. They are asleep in the Adamic Dream: Adam (generic man,) ate of "Maya the tree of illusion" and saw two powers, good and evil.

The Christ mission was to wake people up to the Truth of one Power, God. "Awake thou that sleepeth."

If you lack any good thing, you are still asleep to your good.

How do you awake from the Adamic dream of opposites, after having slept soundly in the race thought for hundreds of years?

Jesus Christ said, "When two of you agree, it shall be done." It is the law of agreement.

It is almost impossible to see clearly, your good, for yourself: that is where the healer, practitioner or friend is necessary.

Many successful men say they have succeeded because their wives believed in them.

I will quote from a current newspaper, giving Walter P. Chrysler's tribute to his wife: "Nothing," he once said, "has given me more satisfaction in life, than the way my wife had faith in me from the very first, through all those years." Chrysler wrote of her, "It seemed to me I could not make any one understand that I was ambitious except

Della. I could tell her and she would nod. It seems to me I even dared to tell her that I intended, some day, to be master mechanic." She always backed his ambitions.

Talk about your affairs as little as possible, and then only to the ones who will give you encouragement and inspiration. The world is full of "Wet blankets," people who tell you "it can't be done," that you are aiming too high.

As people sit in Truth meetings and services, often a word or an idea will open a way in the wilderness.

Of course the Bible is speaking of states of consciousness. You are in a wilderness or desert, when you are out of harmony—when you are angry, resentful, fearful or undecided. Indecision is the cause of much ill health, being unable "to make up your mind."

One day when I was in a bus, a woman stopped it and asked the conductor its destination. He told her, but she was undecided. She got half way on, and then got off, then on again: the conductor turned to her and said, "Lady make up your mind!"

So it is with so many people: "Ladies make up your minds!"

The intuitive person is never undecided: he is given his leads and hunches, and goes boldly ahead, knowing he is on the magic path.

In Truth, we always ask for definite leads just what to do; you will always receive one if you ask for it. Sometimes it comes as intuition, sometimes from the external.

One of my students, named Ada, was walking

down the street, undecided whether to go to a certain place, or not; she asked for a lead. Two women were walking in front of her. One turned to the other and said, "Why don't you go Ada?" — The woman's name just happened to be Ada — my friend took it as a definite lead, and went on to her destination, and the outcome was very successful.

We really lead magic lives, guided and provided for at every step; *if we have ears to hear and eyes that see.*

Of course we have left the plane of the intellect and are drawing from the superconscious, the God within, which says, "This is the way, walk ye in it."

Whatever you should know, will be revealed to you. Whatever you lack, will be provided! "Thus saith the Lord which maketh a way in the sea and a path in the mighty waters."

"Remember ye not the former things, neither consider the things of old."

People who live in the past have severed their contact with the wonderful *now.* God knows only the now; now is the appointed time, today is the day.

Many people lead lives of limitation, hoarding and saving, afraid to use what they have; which brings more lack and more limitation.

I give the example of a woman who lived in a small country town: she could scarcely see to get about, and had very little money. A kind friend took her to an oculist, and presented her with glasses, which enabled her to see perfectly. Sometime later she met her on the street without the glasses. She exclaimed, "Where are your glasses?"

The woman replied, "Well, you don't expect me to hack 'em out by using them every day, do you? I only wear them on Sundays."

You must live in the now and be wide awake to your opportunities.

"Behold, I will do a new thing: now it shall spring forth; shall ye not know it? I will even make a way in the wilderness, and rivers in the desert."

This message is meant for the individual: think of your problem and know that Infinite Intelligence knows the way of fulfillment. I say the *way,* for before you called you were answered. *The supply always precedes the demand.*

God is the Giver and the Gift and now creates His own amazing channels.

When you have asked for the Divine Plan of your life to manifest, you are protected from getting the things that are not in the Divine Plan.

You may think that all your happiness depends upon obtaining one particular thing in life; later on, you praise the Lord that you didn't get it.

Sometimes you are tempted to follow the reasoning mind, and argue with your intuitive leads, suddenly the Hand of Destiny pushes you into your right place; under grace, you find yourself back on the magic path again.

You are now wide awake to your good—you have the ears that hear (your intuitive leads,) and the eyes which see the open road of fulfillment.

The genius within me is released. I now fulfill my destiny.

THE INNER MEANING OF SNOW WHITE AND THE SEVEN DWARFS

I have been asked to give a Metaphysical interpretation of Snow White and the Seven Dwarfs, one of Grimm's Fairy Tales.

It is amazing how this picture, a fairy story, swept sophisticated New York, and the whole country, due to Walt Disney's genius.

This fairy tale was supposed to be for children, but men and women have packed the theatre. It is because fairy tales come down from old legends of Persia, India and Egypt, which are founded on Truth.

Snow White, the little Princess, has a cruel step-mother, who is jealous of her. This cruel step-mother idea appears also in "Cinderalla."

Nearly everyone has a cruel step-mother. THE CRUEL STEP-MOTHER IS A NEGATIVE THOUGHT-FORM YOU HAVE BUILT UP IN THE SUBCONSCIOUS.

Snow White's cruel step-mother is jealous of her and always keeps her in rags and in the background.

ALL CRUEL THOUGHT FORMS DO THIS.

The cruel step-mother consults her magic mirror every day, saying: "Magic mirror on the wall, who is the fairest of them all?" One day the mirror replies: "Thou Queen, mayst fair and beauteous be, but Snow White is lovelier far than thee." This enrages the Queen, so she decides to send Snow White to the forest to be killed by one of her servants. However, the servant's heart melts when Snow White begs for her life, so he leaves her in the woods. The woods are filled with terrifying animals and many pitfalls and dangers. She falls in terror to the ground, and while there, a most unusual spectacle presents itself. Scores of the most delightful little animals and birds creep up and surround her. Rabbits, squirrels, deer, beavers, raccoons, etc. She opens her eyes and greets them with pleasure; they are so friendly and attractive. She tells her story and they lead her to a little house which she makes her home. NOW THESE FRIENDLY BIRDS AND ANIMALS SYMBOLIZE OUR INTUITIVE LEADS OR HUNCHES, WHICH ARE ALWAYS READY TO "GET YOU OUT OF THE WOODS."

The little house proves to be the home of the Seven Dwarfs. Everything is in disorder, so Snow White and her animal friends begin to clean the house. The squirrels dust with their tails, the birds hang things up, using the little deer's horns for a hat-rack. When the seven dwarfs come home from their work of digging gold, they discover the change and at last find Snow White asleep on one of the beds. In the morning she tells her story,

remains with them to keep house and cook their meals, and is very happy. THE SEVEN DWARFS SYMBOLIZE THE PROTECTIVE FORCES ALL ABOUT US.

In the meantime, the cruel step-mother consults her mirror and it says to her: "Over the hills in the green wood shade, where the Seven Dwarfs their dwelling have made, there Snow White is hiding her head, and she, is lovelier far, Oh, Queen than thee." This infuriates the Queen; so she starts off disguised as an old hag, with a poisoned apple for Snow White. She finds her in the house of the Seven Dwarfs and tempts her with the big, red luscious apple. The birds and animals endeavor to tell her not to touch it. THEY TRY TO GIVE HER THE HUNCH NOT TO EAT IT. They rush around in dismay, but Snow White can't resist the apple, she takes one bite and falls, apparently dead. Now all the little birds and animals rush off to bring the Seven Dwarfs to the rescue; but too late, Snow White lies lifeless. They all bow their little heads in grief. Then suddenly the Prince appears, kisses Snow White, and she comes to life. They are married and live happily ever after. The Queen, the cruel step-mother, is swept away by a terrific storm, THE OLD THOUGHT-FORM IS DISSOLVED AND DISSIPATED FOREVER. THE PRINCE SYMBOLIZES THE DIVINE PLAN OF YOUR LIFE. WHEN IT WAKES YOU UP YOU LIVE HAPPILY EVER AFTER.

This is the fairy story which has enthralled New York and the whole country.

Find out what form of tyranny *your* cruel step-mother is taking in *your* subconscious. It is some negative conviction which works out in all your affairs.

We hear people saying: "My good always comes to me too late." "I've lost so many opportunities!" We must reverse the thought and say repeatedly: *"I am wide awake to my good, I never miss a trick."*

WE MUST DROWN OUT THE DREARY SUGGESTIONS OF THE CRUEL STEP-MOTHER. *ETERNAL VIGILANCE IS THE PRICE OF FREEDOM FROM THESE NEGA-TIVE THOUGHT-FORMS.*

Nothing can hinder, nothing can delay the manifestation of the Divine Plan of my life.

The Light of Lights streams on my pathway, revealing the Open Road of Fulfillment!

The Prosperity Wisdom of

Florence Scovel Shinn

Has Been Updated and Improved!

THE COMPLETE WRITINGS OF
FLORENCE SCOVEL SHINN FOR WOMEN
Trade Paperback | 336 pg | 087516-783-7 | $16.95

THE GAME OF LIFE FOR WOMEN
Trade Paperback | 96 pg | 087516-782-9 | $9.95

Although her original work was composed in the prevailing dialect of that time, Shinn's lessons, stories, and insight engaged female readers despite the masculine references. In response to the call from the growing number of women who yearn to connect on a deeper level with her soul-stirring concepts, these beloved writings have now been updated with contemporary references that empower the feminine spirit and allow women to easily relate to the essence of her genuine thoughts.

Now the world's most celebrated books on how to "WIN" the game of life through positive attitudes and affirmations are refined for women, giving them the opportunity to cultivate success and bond closely with Florence Scovel Shinn's everlasting wisdom like never before.

Read the latest *wish* books!